the grove

the grove

a novel

John Rector

Mariner Books · Houghton Mifflin Harcourt

Boston · New York

First Mariner Books edition 2011
Text copyright © 2010 by John Rector

All rights reserved

For information about permission to reproduce selections from this book,
write to Permissions, Houghton Mifflin Harcourt Publishing Company,
215 Park Avenue South, New York, New York 10003.

www.hmhbooks.com

First self-published, in a slightly different form, in 2009
Published in 2010 by AmazonEncore

Library of Congress Cataloging-in-Publication Data is available
ISBN 978-0-547-74498-8

Printed in the United States of American
DOC 10 9 8 7 6 5 4 3 2 1

For Amy, again and always

We live, as we dream—alone . . .

—Joseph Conrad, *Heart of Darkness*

Part One

sunday

1

I had a dream someone was in the house. Then I thought it might not be a dream and I opened my eyes.

The light from the window was bright and drilled into my head. I was in bed, still dressed. My shoes were on, and there were streaks of mud on the sheets. I sat up slowly then heard footsteps in the hallway.

"Morning, Dex."

Greg stood in the doorway, dressed for work. I smiled, not sure why. I was used to seeing him in his uniform, but this time something about the badge struck me as funny.

He had a cup in his hand, and he held it out to me.

"I went ahead and made a pot. Hope you don't mind."

"Why would I mind? It's not like you let yourself in without being invited."

"Suspicion of criminal activity," he said. "If you like, you can file a complaint with the county on Monday."

"There's an idea." I took a drink of the coffee. It was strong, and it burned when I swallowed. "So, what brings you out, Sheriff?"

"Just stopping by."

I didn't think a casual visit was the reason he was here, and I told him so.

"Well, maybe not." Greg stepped toward the window and angled down to look out. "How you feeling? Doing OK?"

"Checking up on me?"

Greg made a low noise in the base of his throat then stepped back from the window and paced the room.

I set the coffee cup on the nightstand next to the empty Johnny Walker bottle. My .22 was there, too, but the clip was gone.

I looked up at Greg.

"You'll get it back, don't worry."

"When?"

"Haven't decided."

I shook my head and went to stand. The floor shifted under me. Greg reached out, but I waved him off and staggered past him to the bathroom in the hall. I closed the door and leaned over the sink and stared at the mirror.

The reflection reminded me of my father.

I ran the water cold and tried to wash away the lines around my eyes, then went back to the bedroom and grabbed my coffee from the nightstand.

I walked down the hallway toward the kitchen. Greg was sitting at the table with the paper open. As I got closer, I saw it was the comics section.

I sat across from him, didn't speak.

"Got a call from Liz this morning," Greg said, not looking up. "Said she came by last night for a few of her things."

"That's right."

"Said there was some kind of incident."

I sipped my coffee.

Greg leaned back, stared at me. "Said you scared her pretty bad, Dex."

I set the cup on the table. "Wasn't my intention."

"The way she tells it, you waved a gun in her face and told her the only good woman was one that wasn't breathing."

That sounded about right, but I kept quiet.

"You don't see how that might've upset her a bit?"

"Jesus, Greg."

"You still taking your pills?"

"What the hell does that have to do with anything?"

"You tell me. I haven't had to come out here like this in years, and you and I both know it's because of those pills. If you stopped taking them, it might explain your behavior last night."

"What behavior?"

Greg crossed his arms over his chest. "Did you black out?"

I looked away.

"What do you remember?"

"I remember some."

My voice came out harsher than I'd wanted. It made me sound defensive, and maybe I was. Greg was trying to rattle me, and it was working. He's always known what buttons to push to get under my skin. He's been doing it since we were kids.

Greg kept staring at me, silent.

"If you got something to say, say it."

He paused. "Where's your tractor, Dex?"

I didn't want to—goddamn it, I didn't want to—but I did anyway. I got up and crossed to the window and looked out at the spot beside the house where I kept the tractor.

It was gone.

"Liz said you threatened to plow your field under. You remember that?"

I shook my head and didn't speak, just stared at the dark oil stains on the gravel where my tractor had been the day before.

Greg started to say something else, but I walked past him and out the back door.

In late summer, when the corn is at its highest, it's impossible to see the entire field from the ground. This time, I didn't need to. There was a wide break in the rows about thirty feet from the house.

I muttered under my breath and headed toward it.

Greg followed me to the break.

"Looks like you made it almost all the way to the grove before running the back end into the ravine. Good thing, too. You can't afford to lose this crop."

I stood at the edge of the corn and stared down the wide scar I'd cut the night before. The path curved a bit, but I only had to take a few steps to see my tractor sitting fifty yards down, tipped up, its back wheels planted in the ravine that ran alongside the cottonwood grove.

Liz had been at me for years to cut those trees out, but I wouldn't do it. She called it wasted land, and I suppose she had a point. The grove cut into the edge of the field, creating a bend that was a hassle come harvest. It would've been much easier to dig it out and be done with it, but I liked it.

The field behind the grove was sheltered and quiet, the cottonwoods on one side and a low line of hills on the other. From back there you couldn't see the house or the road, and better still, no one could see you.

I'd had to throw a few kids out of there from time to time, but I was never angry about it. Growing up in this part of the world was boring, and the grove was a perfect spot to have a couple beers or get high or do whatever else they wanted to do without being seen.

I didn't blame them, but I didn't need them stomping through my field and leaving beer cans and fast food bags behind to attract the rats, either.

I still remembered what it was like being a kid. I just didn't care anymore.

"You gonna want help pulling her out?"

I shook my head. "I'll get her."

Once I said it, I regretted it. There was mud back there, and I knew that would make things tough. And if it rained, tough would become impossible.

"If you change your mind, you can give me a call. I'll bring the truck by. Got a new winch. Wouldn't mind trying her out."

"Thanks. I'll let you know."

He nodded, and for a moment we both just stood there, staring at the tractor. Then Greg spoke.

"You ever think it might be for the best? Her leaving and all?"

He must've read the look on my face because when he spoke again he stumbled over his words.

"I was only thinking of the way things have gone since—" He held up his hands, stopping himself. "Look, Dex, all I'm saying is you two have been through things no couple should have to go through. Maybe a new start, for both of you, is the best—"

I walked away, leaving him alone.

When I got back to the house, I took a beer from the refrigerator then went out to the front porch and sat on one of the wicker chairs Liz had picked up from the county crafts show the year before. A minute later, Greg came around the side of the house and stopped at the bottom of the porch steps. He saw the bottle and shook his head.

"You know it ain't even noon yet?"

"I got nothing planned today."

He looked like he was about to say something else, but I cut him off.

"How about the clip to my gun?"

Greg smiled. "I don't think so, Dex. At least not today."

"When?"

He started toward his cruiser in the driveway. "You can get it at dinner this weekend, if you want to come. Julie would love to see you, same with the boys."

"I don't know."

He reached into his pocket and held up the clip. "That's the price I'm asking."

"I'm pretty sure what you're doing is illegal, Sheriff."

Greg laughed and waved back over his shoulder. He got into the cruiser and backed down the driveway, then turned out onto the road. A thick trail of dust lifted into the air behind him and shone white in the sun before drifting over the cornfield and dissolving in the breeze.

I stayed on the porch and watched his cruiser crest the hill and disappear on the other side.

2

I turned on the shower and stood under the water until it ran cold. There was a dull ache building behind my eyes, and I knew from experience that it was going to get worse before it got better. I tried to remember the last time I'd eaten, but nothing came to me.

When I went into the bedroom to get dressed, I found some pants and a semi-clean shirt on the floor. I slid them on then crossed the room to Liz's closet and opened the door. Most of her clothes were still hanging inside. I ran my hand back and forth along the line of fabric, then stepped back and sat on the edge of the bed.

I sat there for a while, staring into her closet and listening to the sounds of the house.

Empty houses have unique noises, almost like the rooms themselves are listening. The sensation of being observed felt so real that I couldn't pull myself away.

I kept going back to what Greg had said, wondering if Liz and I were better off apart. The more I thought about it, the angrier I felt. I knew Greg wouldn't say anything unless he thought it would help, but I couldn't figure out what the hell he'd been thinking.

Liz and I weren't better off. We were miles from better off, and he knew it.

The pain behind my eyes turned sharp, and I forced myself to get up and head to the kitchen. I needed to eat and to clear my head before going out to the ravine.

I found some ham slices and a can of Cheez Whiz in the refrigerator, and made a sandwich using two crusts of bread. It was all I had in the house. If I wanted to eat again, I'd need to go into town and do some shopping.

The idea killed my appetite, but I ate anyway.

The sandwich was dry, and when I finished it I grabbed a beer. It was enough to keep me going.

I leaned against the counter and closed my eyes. The breeze coming through the window was as gentle as a kiss, and it felt good on my skin.

After a moment I reached for the phone on the wall and held the receiver to my ear and dialed Liz's mother's number. I let it ring once; then hung up.

What was I going to say to her?

If what Greg said was true, if I'd threatened to kill her, what could I say? She'd expect an apology. More than likely she'd want me to beg her for forgiveness, and that wasn't going to happen.

She was the one who'd left me, the one who'd packed up and walked out with no warning, but she didn't care about that, wouldn't even want to talk about that.

No, she would want to talk about my pills, and my

blackouts. Nothing about her. She didn't care about the fog that came with taking the pills, or how the color drained out of everything, a little more every day.

None of that mattered to her.

All she'd want to know was that I was taking them. Nothing else was important. But I wasn't going to deal with that anymore, especially now that she was gone.

I finished my beer and dropped the empty bottle in the sink, then opened the cabinet above the refrigerator and took down a bottle of Johnny Walker. I broke the seal.

The pain in my head faded with each swallow.

The more I thought about Liz, the more I wondered if Greg was right after all. Even if she did come back, things wouldn't be the way they were. She'd told me the night she left that I'd always remind her of Clara.

That wasn't something I could fight.

I took another drink, then capped the bottle and went down the hall to the bedroom. I opened my closet and grabbed a large cardboard box off the top shelf. It was marked "winter" and filled with sweaters. I dumped them on the bed, then opened Liz's closet and started tearing clothes off hangers and throwing them in the box.

I was going to make it easy for her.

For us both.

I'd emptied half the closet before I stopped and looked down at the dress in my hand.

It was like a snapshot.

I could remember her wearing it several times over the years, but right then all I saw was the first time. The

Fourth of July. The night we grilled hamburgers in the backyard and ate outside on the porch and watched the fireworks bloom over the cornfields.

I remembered Clara saying the dress made her look thin and the way Liz laughed and smiled and told her she was a charmer.

I remembered the way she looked crossing the bedroom toward me later that night, the dress moving against her skin like a shadow, fluid and soft and warm.

I sat on the edge of the bed, holding the dress in my lap. There were no tears, but I didn't move from that spot for a long time.

When I did get up, I hung all her clothes back in the closet, one by one, then went outside and crossed the field toward my tractor, still stuck in the ravine.

3

I didn't think anything was broken, but the bleeding wouldn't stop.

I took off my shirt and wrapped the sleeve tight around my hand. I could feel my heart beat under it as I leaned back against the tractor. A slow red stain soaked through the sleeve, and blood pooled in my palm.

I considered going back to the house and driving into town to the medical clinic, but I didn't see the point. It would stop. I hadn't drunk that much, and I could clean my hand when I finished getting the tractor out.

I'd gotten close, even managed to get one of the back wheels free, and I'd almost had the other one out when the board I was using to brace the tire snapped and dug into my hand. It wasn't until I saw the blood running down my arm that I realized what had happened.

I hadn't felt a thing.

I shook the blood out of my palm then unwrapped it and rewrapped it with the other sleeve. The bleeding seemed to be slowing, and I felt better about not going back to the house. The day was already slipping away, and I didn't want to stop just because of a little scratch.

With my hand wrapped tight again, I looked around for another board or rock I could use to brace the tire in the mud. I didn't see anything, so I climbed up the far side of the ravine and walked into the cottonwoods.

The air in the grove felt ten degrees cooler. I stopped in the middle of the trees and glanced up at the shimmer of leaves rattling in the breeze. The sound was calming, and I stood for a while just listening and breathing and watching the early evening light filter through the branches.

I noticed a few empty beer cans on the ground and kicked a couple of them into a pile in case I decided to come out later and pick them up.

It was a ridiculous thought. I kept searching.

Something on the other side of the grove caught my eye. I didn't recognize it at first. When I got closer I saw that it was a purse, striped pink and blue, like ribbon candy. I picked it up. There was weight to it, and I looked around to see if anyone was there. I knew I was alone, but something in me needed to make sure.

I examined the purse. It was unmarked and looked brand new. I set it on the ground, unsnapped the latch, and checked inside.

The first thing I saw was a smaller bag, the same design. There were several makeup tubes inside.

I reached back into the purse and came out with a few pens, a checkbook, a wallet.

I opened the checkbook. The bank was local, and according to the registry the balance in the account was twenty-seven dollars and change. I dropped it back in the purse, then grabbed the wallet and took out the driver's license.

The girl in the license photo had dark hair pulled back into a ponytail. She was young and she was smiling. Her name was Jessica Cammon. I read the date of birth and did the math in my head.

She was sixteen.

I looked around at the scattering of beer cans and shook my head. If I found out my sixteen-year-old daughter had been drinking in secluded cornfields—

I stopped myself.

After a moment I thumbed through the rest of the wallet. There were thirteen dollars inside and several pay stubs. I pulled one out and read the name: The Riverbank Café.

I'd been to the Riverbank Café several times. I looked closer at the driver's license photo, wondering if I'd seen her there. I couldn't place the face, but it was a long time since I'd been there. Maybe she was new.

I slid the license back into the wallet and returned it to the purse. I thought about going to the Riverbank Café for breakfast tomorrow. Going there would keep me out of the grocery store for another day. Besides, it would be fun to see the look on her face when I dropped her purse on the counter.

I knew what I should do was take it to the address on the license and hand it over to her parents. Tell them where I found it and let them handle the situation. But it wasn't any of my business. I figured I should just find her and return the purse.

Her parents could ask the questions.

I snapped the bag closed without looking at anything else. The sun was beginning its slow drop toward the horizon, and soon the sky would fill with a heavy red haze.

If I didn't get back to the tractor soon I'd have no choice but to finish tomorrow. If that happened, I figured I'd call Greg and tell him to bring his truck out after all. We'd have it done in twenty minutes.

I started back toward the ravine, taking one last look over my shoulder. When I did, I noticed something lying in the corn just past the trees, but I couldn't tell what it was from where I stood.

I moved toward it.

The wind had picked up, and whatever it was danced back and forth in the breeze. It looked like a dark jacket or a shirt caught in the corn.

I crossed the grove and stepped out into the sheltered area just past the trees. Taking a few steps closer, I stopped.

What I'd seen was a waitress uniform from the Riverside Café, a black dress with a gold stripe running along the hem. I recognized it immediately.

The girl wearing the dress was on her side facing into the field, away from where I stood. Her dark hair was matted to her head, and her legs were folded up toward her chest as if she were sleeping. One arm was stretched out in front of her and the other was down along her side, the palm facing the sky.

Even without seeing her face, I knew.

4

When I got back to the house, I was out of breath and covered in mud. I'd fallen in the ravine and hit my head on a half-buried rock. I could feel the steady warm flow of blood running down my cheek.

I ran to the kitchen, dialed Greg's number, and let it ring. There was no answer. I hung up. I looked at the clock above the stove. It was almost eight. I doubted he'd still be at work, but even if he wasn't, they could track him down.

I didn't want to talk to anyone else.

I opened the cabinet where Liz kept the phone book and pulled it out, scanning the first few pages for the Sheriff's Department. When I found the number I picked up the phone and started to dial.

Halfway through, I stopped.

Why would I only talk to Greg?

A thought flashed in the back of my mind, brief but sharp. It wouldn't let me call.

It happened again.

I stood in the kitchen, blood on my face and the

phone pressed against my ear, unable to move, trying to push the thought away.

"No."

My voice was soft, a whisper against the receiver.

The thought flashed again, and this time there were images, bad images. I tried to close my eyes, but it didn't help.

It happened again.

It wasn't possible.

The girl hadn't been out there for very long, that was obvious, but that didn't mean she'd been out there last night. It didn't mean that I'd seen her and confronted her, or that I'd—

No, it wasn't possible.

I closed my eyes and tried to bring back anything from the night before. All I had was a confusing haze of images and words, then nothing until I woke up that morning covered in mud.

It happened again.

The thought was enough to move my hand holding the phone back toward the cradle.

I crossed the room to the refrigerator and grabbed a beer. I opened it and took a drink, then held the cold bottle against my forehead.

When I pulled it away, it was bloody.

I reached for the towel over the sink and ran it under cold water, then pressed it against my forehead, wincing.

I'd caught kids in my field before, but I'd never been angry about it. All I'd ever done was ask them to leave. No fights, no problems.

But how would this look?

Greg and I had been friends since grade school, and thanks to my father's drinking, I'd spent more time at his house than my own. He'd been there through all the bad times, and we were as close as brothers. But finding a dead body on my property the day after I'd waved a gun at my wife and threatened to kill her wouldn't look good.

He'd have questions, and not just him.

A lot of people would look to me, and everything from the past would come up again.

I wished I'd never gone out there.

I considered waiting it out, pretending I'd never found the body. I didn't think I had anything to do with the girl, and since no one else knew I'd been out there or what I'd found, all I had to do was keep quiet.

I thought about it for a minute, but inside I knew it wasn't an option. I had to call.

Whatever followed would follow.

I went back to the counter and reached for the phone to call Greg. Before I could pick it up, it rang.

I didn't move.

My throat was tight, and I felt my heart drill against my ribs. After the fourth ring, I picked it up.

"Hi, Dexter."

It was Liz.

I carried the phone to the table, sat down, then leaned back in the chair and closed my eyes. Each second that passed I cursed myself for not saying anything, but the words wouldn't come.

"How are you feeling?"

"I'm OK."

The wind blew the curtain back from the window, and I glanced up and saw the grove in the distance. I looked down at my hands on the table, saw the dried blood under my fingernails, and squeezed a fist.

"What do you need, Liz?"

"Same thing I needed last night. Half my clothes are sitting in the closet over there, all my books—"

"Come get them, I won't stop you."

"That's what you said before."

"Yeah," I said. "I guess I did."

I heard the unmistakable scratch of a cigarette lighter followed by a long exhale.

"When did you go off your medication?"

"When did you start smoking again?"

She didn't answer, and for a moment neither of us said a word. After a while, Liz spoke.

"That's a serious decision, Dexter."

"I don't owe you an explanation. You're the one who walked away."

"Is that what this is about? I leave so you stop your pills? How long have you been off them? A week? Two weeks?"

"It's none of your business."

"It's cowardly, that's what it is." She exhaled into the phone. "You think you're the only one who lost something in all of this?"

She didn't wait for me to answer.

"Clara was my daughter, too, and I feel it every day,

as much as you, but that never enters your head. Nothing matters to you except you."

I kept quiet.

"I tried to keep things together with us," Liz said. "You can't say I didn't try."

"You didn't try that hard."

"I tried as hard as I could."

"It wasn't enough."

Silence.

"What did you do, Dexter? Did *you* try?"

I didn't answer her. I tried to remember the sound of Clara's voice. It was getting harder to do these days.

"I'm sorry," I said.

"For what?"

Liz's voice sounded tired. I knew whatever answer I gave wouldn't matter, so I kept it to myself.

She waited for me to say something. When I didn't, she said, again, "I need to pick up my things."

"Do you remember the bracelets? The ones she made out of all that string?"

"Dexter."

"I lost every one she gave me." I laughed. "She must've made hundreds of those goddamn things. Used to find them all over the house, but now I can't find one of them. I've looked everywhere, under furniture, rugs. Not one."

"Dexter."

"Hard to believe there's not a pile of them lying in the corner of some closet somewhere."

"I have a couple."

"They were all over the place, and now—"

"I can give you one."

I ran the back of my hand across my cheek. "I've looked everywhere."

"I'll give you one of mine."

I paused. "I'm sorry about last night. I promise it'll be OK next time."

"It would be better if I came by when you weren't around. I'm not sure it's a good idea to see you right now."

"Why?"

"Do you really have to ask?"

"It was a bad night, that's all."

She started to say something, then stopped. "Do you remember last night at all?"

"I know what I did."

She paused. The next time she spoke, her voice was quiet.

"Did you black out?"

"I told you, I know what I did."

"That's serious, Dexter, you know that."

I felt the anger build in my chest, and it took an effort to push it back.

"I wouldn't have hurt you."

"How do you know? How do I know? You're not on your pills, and if you're blacking out you have no idea what you might do."

"Liz."

"Did you forget what can happen?"

"It's none of your goddamn business."

I heard her take the phone away and then the sound of her crushing out her cigarette. When she came back to the phone, her voice was calm.

"OK, it's none of my business, but you didn't see how you were acting last night, and I did. I haven't seen you like that since—" She paused. "In years."

I let that sink in, then said, "Can I ask you something?"

"I don't know."

"Do you think I could've hurt someone last night? Really hurt someone?"

She didn't answer right away, and I could tell she was choosing her words carefully. After a moment, she said, "You scared me last night. You were a different person."

"But do you think I could've—"

"Yes," she said. "I do."

5

I didn't call Greg.

After Liz hung up, I stayed in the kitchen and stared out the window at the darkening field and the cotton-wood grove in the distance. I thought about what she had said.

I had no memory of the previous night, that was true, but I knew with every part of me that I hadn't hurt any-one. I didn't know how the girl wound up in my field, or who'd killed her, but I was sure it had nothing to do with me.

Still, once the news got out and people in town heard where they'd found the girl's body, the rumors would be everywhere.

No one around here forgets.

Over the years I'd become accustomed to the stares and whispers when I went into town. They'd tapered off since Clara but never completely stopped. All it would take to bring them back was a spark.

Like another murder.

I got up and took the Johnny Walker bottle from the cabinet above the refrigerator, then went outside to sit on the porch. The sun was almost gone, and the sky was red and heavy. There were several dark clouds to the east trailing thin blue curtains of rain. I sat on the steps and drank.

Lightning flashed, and I thought about my tractor. It was going to get wet sitting in the ravine, but there wasn't anything I could do. Calling Greg to help wasn't a good idea. We went back a long time, but if he thought I had anything to do with the girl's death, everything we'd been through together wouldn't matter.

Telling him wasn't an option unless I could prove that I wasn't involved.

I took another drink and watched the cottonwoods in the grove fight against the wind.

Could I prove it? There had to be something out there that pointed away from me, something I'd missed. If I could find it and give it to Greg, then I could show him—

No, that was a bad idea.

Anything I'd come across, someone with training would also find. I'd just make a mess out there, probably without accomplishing a thing.

Still, the idea wouldn't go away.

Bad ideas rarely do, with me.

When we were kids, Greg fell out of an oak tree we'd been climbing in front of his house and snapped his leg in two places. I remember seeing the bone sticking through the skin and knowing I had to do something. His parents weren't home at the time, so I ended up carrying him for two miles on my back to Dr. Whitfield's house for help.

When we finally got there, Dr. Whitfield braced Greg's leg and drove us both down to the hospital. I stayed in the waiting room until Greg's parents arrived. When they did, I told them what'd happened.

I exaggerated Greg's injury and the difficulty of carrying him all that way to make myself sound more heroic. When I finished the story, I was beaming.

Greg's father looked down at me, frowning. "Why the hell didn't you call from the house? Why do all that for no reason?"

I didn't have an answer.

When we got to see Greg, his parents commended him on his bravery and told him how proud they were of him for enduring the pain of being carried so far with a broken leg.

I kept quiet.

Later, back at his house and alone, Greg thanked me.

"I would've done the same thing," he'd said. "I didn't think of the phone either. Don't let it bother you."

I didn't believe him. Greg was always good under pressure. Greg was always good at everything. That's just the way things were.

Me? I was the crazy one with the alcoholic father. It wasn't until high school, when I'd learned I could hit a baseball better than anyone else, that people began to notice me for something positive, and eventually things got better.

I met Liz, I had scholarship offers from several schools, but best of all, I stopped being Donald McCray's messed-up kid for a while.

Then everything crumbled.

And now it was all crumbling again.

No, I couldn't call Greg, and yes, investigating the girl's death was a bad decision, but it was the only one I could see.

I capped the bottle of Scotch and slid it into my pocket then started for the break in the rows of corn that led out to the grove.

I thought again about my new plan and wondered if going off my pills might be affecting my judgment.

I didn't like the answer that came to me, but in the end, I decided it really didn't matter.

6

The girl was on her side, facing the corn. Her hair, falling over her face like a veil, shimmered with movement. As I got closer I saw the flies, thick and black, covering the ground by her head.

I stepped over her and the flies scattered, revealing a dried yellow trail of vomit running into the dirt. There was no blood that I could see, and her uniform looked clean, no rips or stains.

I waved more flies away, then bent over and ran a finger along the girl's forehead. I wanted to push her hair back from her face, but it was stuck to the dried vomit on her skin. The sound of it tearing free made my throat clench.

The flies gathered around my feet as I knelt over the girl. Her lips were purple and cracked. One of her eyes was half-closed; the other, milky and gray, stared toward the sky. The black makeup under her eyes had clumped into the lashes and smeared against her pale blue skin, making her look as though she'd been crying.

Once again, I slid a finger along her forehead, looping her hair behind her ear. There were three small silver rings in her earlobe and another through the cartilage at the top.

When I pulled my hand away, the back of my fingers brushed across her cheek. I'd expected her skin to be cold, but it wasn't. The sun, which had now dropped just below the horizon, had kept her warm, but with night coming, that would change.

I balanced on the balls of my feet and looked over the ground around her. Nothing stood out.

There was a red ant crawling in the upturned palm of her right hand. I reached down and squeezed it between my fingers, then tossed it aside. When I did, I noticed a class ring on the middle finger of her right hand. It was too big for her, and she'd wrapped tape around the underside of the band to make it fit.

I leaned in closer and saw a football and goalposts embossed on one side and on the other the initials JHS.

Jefferson High School.

I had one exactly like it back in the house, except mine had an embossed baseball and an American flag.

I had never let anyone wear it.

I leaned in and tried to get a better look at her face. I'd seen the photo on her driver's license, but it wasn't enough.

Reaching for her shoulder, I hesitated.

Moving her would look bad. I tried to think of excuses I could use if anyone ever found out.

I could say I wanted to see if she was really dead. It was as good an excuse as any, and good enough for me.

I turned her over.

I'd heard that when you die your body becomes

heavy, but when I rolled her onto her back it felt like she wasn't there at all.

After I moved her, I had to look away.

The left side of her face was a deep black where the blood had settled, and the arm that'd been out in front of her now pointed over her head. I was able to pull it down to her side, but when I did, the muscles popped with the movement.

Her legs, still bent at the knee, now peaked toward the sky. The angle made her skirt slide up toward her waist, exposing thin blue panties underneath.

I reached down and pulled the hem of her skirt toward her knees. It wouldn't stay, so I pressed down on both her legs until they were straight.

This time, the skirt stayed down, and I ignored the twinge in my stomach, the growing tightness in my pants.

Thin blue panties?

I looked down at her face and tried to piece together what had happened to her, how she'd wound up in my field.

Lightning flashed in the east, and I felt the first few touches of rain on my skin. I looked up and saw the clouds coming in fast. If I was going to find anything, I needed to hurry.

I took another look around but didn't see anything unusual. I noticed the purse again. It was sitting on the edge of the grove by the cottonwoods, right where I'd dropped it after I'd first found her.

I thought there might've been something I'd missed the first time, a connection or clue that I'd passed over when I didn't know to look.

I picked up the purse and unsnapped the latch. A small green case sat on the bottom. I took it out and opened it. Inside were several tampons. I closed the case and dropped it back in the purse, then reached for the bottle in my pocket, unscrewed the cap, and took a drink.

A few minutes later I tried again.

I found a black address book closed with a Velcro strip. I opened it and thumbed through the pages. They were all blank. There was a zipper compartment on the side. I looked in and found two photographs. The first one was of Jessica and two other girls I didn't recognize. They were standing outside in the sun, smiling and laughing. All three wore sunglasses and small shirts with wire-thin straps.

The other photograph was of Jessica with a kid who looked a few years older. They were leaning against a black and silver Ford Mustang. Jessica had her arms around his neck and her head against his chest. Neither of them was looking at the camera, or smiling. I assumed the photo was meant to be serious.

In high school, love was serious.

I set the photos between my feet and went back to the purse. I found a pack of Juicy Fruit gum, four pens, and a tin of Altoids. There was some loose change in the bottom along with a business card for a temp agency. The copy on the card said

ACE STAFFING: Call today, work today

I tried to imagine what kind of high school student worked two jobs. Did she need money that bad? Could that have had something to do with her death?

I looked at the photographs one more time, wondering if anyone even knew she was gone.

A raindrop landed on one of the pictures, and I wiped it away with my thumb. The sky had turned from red to purple to black. I knew if I didn't want to get wet, it was time to go.

Tomorrow, I decided, I'd go into town and see what I could find out about Jessica Cammon. Someone had to know what had happened.

I took one more look at the photo, studying Jessica's face, and imagined her wrapping her arms around my neck, hugging me and thanking me for helping her.

It made me smile.

I put the photos back and closed the purse, leaving it where I'd found it, then turned away from the grove and headed toward the house. When I crossed the ravine, I looked back. For a moment I felt bad leaving her outside in the rain, but I forced myself to keep walking.

The wind pushed and fought, and the corn surged around me. I walked faster, then ran, and when I reached the house I was out of breath.

A sharp cramp dug into my side. I took the bottle out of my pocket and drank, waiting for the pain to pass.

It went away, but the wind never stopped.

I stood on the porch and stared out at the shadows of the cottonwoods in the grove. The sky was now completely dark, and the rain was coming down hard. I had to remind myself that she'd be all right out there, but something inside me didn't believe it.

She was alone, like me, and for a moment, through the rain, I heard someone crying in the distance.

Then nothing.

I listened for a while longer, then turned and went inside, locking the door behind me.

monday

7

The Riverbank Café was a one-level brick building on the far end of Main Street, windowless except for three small squares of glass on either side of the door. Originally it had been a bar, but the old owner retired and left it to his nephew, who'd turned it into a restaurant.

Apparently, the nephew had found Jesus after running into some trouble with drugs in the city. He'd decided a small business in an even smaller town would go a long way toward healing his soul and saving his marriage.

As long as the business wasn't a bar.

So, the Riverbank Café opened nowhere near a river.

Liz told me once that the name had something to do with John the Baptist, but I'd never been one for fables, and if I'd heard the story I didn't remember it. She'd said, "He was the guy who baptized Jesus then got beheaded by the Romans."

I'd told her they made good omelets.

That had been the end of the conversation.

. . .

I pulled into the dirt lot in front of the Riverbank Café and parked next to a black Wentworth truck pulling a cattle car. Inside, pigs shuffled and grunted in the heat. The grill of the truck was a spray of dead bugs covering a confederate flag.

I got out, crossed the parking lot to the front door, and went inside. The air in the café was cold and felt good on my skin. The woman behind the counter looked up and smiled. There was a flash of recognition behind her eyes, but to her credit, the smile didn't fade.

"Back from the dead, I see," she said. "Just you today, or is your wife coming?"

"Just me," I said.

She nodded, then motioned toward a line of booths along the wall. "Well, sit anywhere you like."

The only people inside were an old couple in one of the booths and a guy in a Harley Davidson T-shirt sitting at the counter. I sat in the corner where I could see the entire room. A minute later a young girl came out of the kitchen, took a menu from the front counter, and crossed over to me.

"Coffee?"

I nodded and took the menu, even though I knew what I wanted.

The girl turned, and I watched her walk away. She didn't look much older than Jessica, but it was hard to tell if she was one of the girls in the photograph or not. If she'd been wearing sunglasses, maybe.

I dropped the menu on the table and leaned back in the booth. Country music drifted through the cook's window into the dining room. The woman behind the counter was refilling ketchup bottles and humming along to a song I'd never heard.

The old man in the booth leaned across the table toward the old woman and whispered something. The old woman giggled then covered her mouth with her napkin. The sound was light and young.

A few minutes later, the waitress came with my coffee and set it on the table. "You know what you want?"

The tag on her uniform said her name was Megan. I handed her the menu and said, "Denver omelet, please, Megan."

She nodded, scribbled on her notepad, then took the menu from me and smiled. "Be right up."

She turned to go and I stopped her. "Where's the other girl who works here?"

"The other girl?" Megan bit her lower lip and glanced over her shoulder toward the woman wiping the counter. The woman didn't look up.

"Long, dark hair," I said. "Haven't seen her around much."

Megan tapped her pen on her notepad then said, "That's Jessica. She's not here today."

"Not here, but she should be," the woman at the counter said. "She might just find herself without a job soon."

"That's too bad," I said. "She seemed nice."

Megan looked from me to the woman behind the counter then disappeared into the kitchen. I heard her say something and a man's voice answer. His head appeared in the cook's window; then it was gone.

"That's the trouble with hiring kids," the woman

said. "They have their own priorities, and most of them don't understand the meaning of hard work. They're too distracted these days."

"That so?" I sipped my coffee, tried to appear disinterested. "Was Jessica easily distracted?"

The woman laughed. "Boys, boys, boys with her, and that's that." She tapped her finger against her chest. "I grew up with four sisters—I know how girls can be, but that one is something else."

"A lot of boyfriends?"

"Not a lot." She capped one of the ketchup bottles and reached for another as she spoke. "One in particular, but at that age, one's enough." She shook her head. "Her poor mother called here yesterday wondering if she'd shown up for her shift. I had to tell her no, but I left it at that. What else am I going to say? 'Sorry, Mrs. Cammon, but your daughter ran off with her boyfriend?'"

"Ran off? You think so?"

She shrugged. "Oh, I don't know, but it wouldn't surprise me a bit."

The man at the counter in the Harley Davidson T-shirt looked over his shoulder at me, then back at the woman. "You don't want a daughter these days, that's for sure."

"I wouldn't say that," the woman said. "Boys can be just as bad."

The man shook his head. "That ain't true. With a boy you only got one dick to worry about." He turned back and smiled at me, his mouth full of chewed egg. "With a girl, you worry about 'em all." He laughed, loud and rolling.

I did, too, just to be polite.

"Ben, don't come in here and be crude." She leaned over and brushed his arm with her hand. "You know better than that."

"Just telling the truth as I see it."

The woman smiled and shook her head. "Well, keep it to yourself."

After that, the topic switched to the weather and how thankful they were for the rain considering how dry it'd been. When Ben started talking about having to haul the load of pigs to the packing plant in Clarksville, I dropped out of the conversation and thought about Jessica.

This had been one of her places. She'd spent time here, walking these floors, cleaning these same tables. I'm not one to believe in ghosts, but I felt like a part of her was still there in that room.

If I tried, I thought I could see her come through the doors leading from the kitchen, each hand holding a plate of food. I glanced up and waited.

A moment later the doors opened and she was there.

Her black hair tied in a ponytail, her skin warm and pink. She crossed the room toward me.

I closed my eyes. My chest felt tight, and I couldn't catch my breath. I kept my eyes closed until I heard the plate touch the table in front of me, then looked up.

Megan took a bottle of ketchup and a bottle of Tabasco from her apron pocket and set them on the table.

"You need anything else right now?"

I stared at my plate and a single chunk of ham, pink and steaming, trapped in the yellow omelet.

My stomach twisted.

"You doing OK?"

I nodded. The last thing I wanted was to come into town and draw attention to myself. I squeezed my fists tight, then looked up and smiled.

"Doing fine, thanks."

Megan hesitated, then said, "If you need anything else, just yell."

She started toward the old couple in the booth, but the woman behind the counter stopped her.

"What's your opinion? You think Jess ran off with her boyfriend?"

Inside, I thanked her.

The girl didn't say anything for a moment; then she looked back at the kitchen and the man watching through the cook's window.

"I—I guess I don't know."

"If anyone knows, it'll be you," the woman said. "I know you two talked."

"I don't think she would've run off. I mean, she didn't mention it to me."

The woman looked at me then pointed at the girl. "Secretive as cats, all of 'em."

The man in the kitchen cleared his throat and said, "Megan, give me a hand with something."

Megan slipped into the kitchen.

This time I didn't hear them talking, and I made a note of it.

"Well, one thing's for sure," the woman said. "When she does show her face again, she's going to have a lot of questions to answer."

I looked down at my omelet. The smell settled in the back of my throat, and something bitter rolled up to meet it. I had to eat. I couldn't come in and order a meal and then leave it untouched, especially not after asking all kinds of questions. People would remember.

I picked at the eggs, then took a bite. At first I thought it was going to come back up, but I forced it to stay down. A few minutes later I tried again. This time it was easier.

The old couple paid their bill and walked, arm in arm, out to the parking lot.

"Sweet," the woman said after they'd gone. "Been married forever and still holding hands."

I ignored her and cut into the omelet. When I'd finished most of it, I folded my napkin over the rest and leaned back. The woman called for Megan, who came out and handed me my bill.

"Didn't mean to put you on the spot," I said.

She smiled, and I thought it was the fakest smile I'd ever seen.

"You didn't at all," she said. "Can I get you anything else?"

"You working all day?"

She shook her head. "Just through lunch." She picked up my plate and waited, then said. "More coffee or anything?"

I shook my head and reached for my wallet.

"Thanks for coming in." She gave me the same smile again and walked away.

I dropped a couple bucks on the table then took the

bill to the front counter. The woman rang me up, and I told her they made the best omelets I'd ever tasted.

She thanked me, then said, "Bring your wife next time. We haven't seen you two together for quite a while."

I nodded. "I'll definitely do that," I said.

And I almost meant it.

8

Louie's Liquors didn't open until eleven o'clock. I parked my truck across the street and sat with the windows down, watching the traffic. At exactly eleven, a neon OPEN sign blinked on in the window. I crossed the street to the front door and went inside.

I came out with eight bottles of Johnny Walker and a case of Budweiser. I put all of it on the floor in front of the passenger seat, then took one of the Johnny Walker bottles from the bag.

It was ten after eleven and I figured Megan wouldn't get off work for a few hours. If I wanted to see where she went, who she saw, and what she did, I'd have to wait. And judging by the way she'd acted in the café, I had a good idea she knew something.

I considered going home for a few hours until her shift ended, but if I did I knew there was a chance I wouldn't make it back to town.

I thought about my options for a while then capped the bottle, started my truck, and pulled out of the parking lot.

• • •

Jefferson High School was less than a mile away.

I'd driven by hundreds of times over the years, but I hadn't set foot on campus since I'd left school halfway through my senior year. I drove around the main building and parked in the senior lot next to the baseball diamond. I got out and looked over the field.

The scoreboard above centerfield was new, but the logo was the same as it had always been—a blue and white bear paw. The Jefferson Bears. There were metal stands on either side of the field and wooden ones built in behind home plate. The field was green and the dirt was red and it all shone clean under a bright yellow sun.

I grabbed my bottle and crossed the parking lot to the gate. It was locked, so I followed the fence along the stands and down toward left field. The fence was lower there, and I climbed over without a problem.

I stayed by the fence for a moment, taking it all in, then crossed to center field and got down on one knee. I ran my hand over the top of the grass.

I had a feeling that no time had passed, that I'd never left. I looked around. Except for the years with Liz and Clara, this was where I'd been happiest. Now, all of that was gone, and coming back was like visiting a graveyard.

I pushed myself up, and crossed toward first base, my position, and stood in my old spot. The bag wasn't out, but the foul lines were chalked and the dirt under my feet felt familiar and good.

I stared up at the stands, remembering how they'd looked when they were full. In small communities, any home game is an event, and sometimes it seemed like the entire town came out to watch us play.

Now, everything was silent, but in my head I could still hear the chaos.

I took the bottle from my pocket and took a drink. The sun felt warm on my neck. I lay back and let myself sink into the grass.

Above me, the sky was a perfect blue.

I could hear the crowds in the stands, cheering me on. I closed my eyes and imagined Jessica sitting out there among them, surrounded by her friends, laughing and joking, completely unaware of what was coming.

The way it should've been.

The image felt so real and so peaceful. It was like a warm wave covering me and pushing me along, farther and farther away from the shore.

. . .

"Number twenty-one, Dexter McCray."

I look around the dugout, but I'm alone. There are people on the field, and the sky behind them is a swirl of red and gray. I hear the announcer again, and this time I get up and climb out to the field.

The stands are full. People are on their feet. I can see them clapping and cheering, but the sound is covered by the wind and the thunder in the distance.

There are bats lined up in front of the dugout. I pick one

up and move toward the on-deck circle. Someone grabs my arm.
I turn around. Clara looks up at me and shakes her head. She
is wearing her white bicycle helmet and a long-sleeved pink top
with a yellow sunflower design in the middle.

"You can't use that one," she says, motioning to the bat.
"It's not fair."

I look down. The wood feels good in my hands.

"What should I use?"

Clara turns and runs back to the dugout, disappearing
down the steps. When she comes back she's carrying a long black
tire iron. She holds it out to me.

"This," she says.

I take the tire iron and let the bat drop to the ground. The
metal is cold and heavy. I start to turn away, then stop and look
back.

"I need a helmet."

She unstraps her bicycle helmet and hands it to me. I slide
it on and head for the batter's box.

The umpire is standing behind the plate. He's staring at
me, but I can't see his face, only a swirling gray void behind the
mask.

I look back toward Clara, but she's gone. Instead, Jessica
is sitting in the stands right above the spot where Clara was.
She's wearing sunglasses and her black and gold uniform from
the café.

She sees me and waves.

I wave back and smile.

"You ready or not, McCray?"

I look out at the players in the field—more empty faces—
then down at the tire iron in my hands.

"I'm ready," I say.

"Then play ball."

The catcher adjusts his stance, the umpire crouching behind him. I raise the tire iron over my shoulder and wait for the pitch.

It comes fast—too fast, catching me in the side of the head. The pain is white and everywhere and I drop to the ground.

No one moves to help.

I stare up at a heavy, rolling sky, the color of blood and ashes.

Someone screams, far off, and then I close my eyes. When I open them again, Jessica is kneeling over me. Her sunglasses are gone and her eyes are dark and swollen.

"I'll help you," she says. "Don't worry."

I look over and see Clara's helmet on the ground next to me. It is cracked. There is blood on the white surface.

"Is that mine?"

Jessica puts a finger to my lips. "Quiet now," she says. "None of that matters anymore."

She's wrong about that, and I want to tell her she's wrong, but the words don't come.

Jessica leans in close and whispers to me.

"I'm here now."

Her words are soft and sweet and as smooth as silver. When I look into her face I see my reflection in her eyes and I can't look away, no matter how hard I try.

• • •

"Hey."

Something hard was pressing against my ribs.

I opened my eyes. For a moment I didn't know where I was; then it all came back.

"You can't be out here," the voice said. "What the hell are you thinking?"

The man was old and bent. He had a key ring in one hand and a broom in the other. He tapped the handle against my chest as he spoke.

"There ain't no kids around, thank God, but this is still a school. You can't come here and drink. A man should know better than to do something like that." He waved his free hand in the air, shooing me away. "Don't make me call the police, now. Go."

"Sorry," I said, pushing myself up. "I used to go here. I just wanted to see—"

"I don't care nothing about any of that." He stared at me as he spoke, and then his eyes went wide. It was a look I'd seen before.

He knew me, and he was scared of me.

"You need to get out of here now," the old man said. "I'll call the police, you understand me?"

I understood fine.

I grabbed my bottle and walked back across left field to the fence. I could still hear Jessica's voice in my head, and I tried to hold on to it. There was such warmth in her voice. I didn't want it to slip away.

At the edge of the field, I looked back. The old man was still standing by first base, staring at me. I waved to him, then slid the bottle into my back pocket and pushed myself up and over the fence.

As I was going, my foot slipped and I went down, landing hard on my back. The fall knocked the wind out of my lungs. I felt the bottle crunch under me, and a cool wetness spread around my waist.

I rolled onto my side and curled into a ball, waiting for my breath to come back. When it did, I braced myself against the fence and got to my feet. A river of whiskey ran down my leg and into the dirt.

The old man was still watching me.

I raised my hand and yelled, "I'm OK."

He turned away, moving slowly toward the stands.

I walked along the fence to the parking lot then out to my truck. When I got there I undid my pants and stepped out of them. They were soaked from the waist to the knees. I pulled the bigger pieces of glass from the back pocket, then crumpled the pants into a ball and tossed them in the back end of the truck.

I heard the gate open and turned around. The old man stepped out. He looked at me, standing by my truck in my underwear, and shook his head.

I started to explain, but he ignored me.

I watched him lock the gate and cross the parking lot toward the main building. When he got there he took his key ring and unlocked the tall glass door, then turned back and waved again.

"Go on, get out."

His voice was thin at that distance.

I waved back.

My boxer shorts were soaked through, and I didn't want to get in the truck with them on. I had two choices. In the end, I slipped them off and tossed them in the back with my pants before driving away.

I started toward home, glancing at the clock on

my dashboard. It was past one o'clock. If I went home, I wouldn't make it back in time to follow Megan. But I was naked from the waist down, so I kept driving.

I wasn't sure how long the lunch shift lasted or if she was already gone. I figured I should at least drive by and check. If she was still there, it would be an opportunity I couldn't pass up.

The smell of whiskey was thick in the cab. If I got pulled over, I'd have a lot to explain. I looked down and shook my head.

I could hear Jessica laughing.

"It's not funny," I said, but she didn't stop. The sound made me smile, and soon I was laughing with her.

9

When I got to the Riverside Café, Megan was sitting on the steps out front. She had a book open on her lap and didn't look up when I drove by. A block down the road I doubled back then parked across the street and watched.

Jessica's voice was buzzing in my head. No words, just a low steady pulse of mumbles and noise. I tried my best to push the sounds away, but my thoughts seemed to go by too fast, one after the other. I couldn't slow them down.

I leaned over and grabbed a new bottle from the floor in front of the passenger seat. My hand wavered, but I managed to open it and get it to my lips. I concentrated on each movement, talking myself through it. *Lift, drink, swallow, breathe. Lift, drink, swallow, breathe.*

I knew if I focused, I'd be able to slow my mind down long enough to stop the voices. An old trick, one that I'd used when things got bad, before I had my pills.

Sometimes it worked.

When I was younger, the voice I'd heard most often was my father's. It would scream through me, ripping and destroying. Jessica's voice was different, soothing. I wanted to drown in it, and that was almost as bad.

I'd been on the medication for so long I'd forgotten how easy it was to let it all get away from me.

I kept my focus, and slowly Jessica's voice faded and I began to feel calm. I leaned back and closed my eyes, taking in the silence. When things felt normal again, I took another drink.

I tried not to think about how easily her voice had slid into my mind, how comfortable it had felt, how safe. Instead, I turned my attention back to Megan.

She was still on the steps, reading. She never looked up from the book. Five minutes passed, then ten. I wondered who she was waiting for. Then I saw a black and silver Ford Mustang pull into the parking lot and stop in front of the café.

Megan closed her book. She crossed the parking lot to the car and leaned into the passenger window. A moment later she opened the door and got inside. The Mustang circled around and pulled out onto the road.

I watched it for about a block, then followed.

It was the same car in the photograph, and part of me couldn't believe it. I'd seen the stories of teenage murder plots in the news, but I'd never expected to see one around here.

Greg told me once that when someone is murdered the killer is almost always someone the victim knows.

But why kill her?

I followed the Mustang down Main Street. The car slowed at Ridge Road before turning left and heading toward the wildlife refuge by the river. There were no houses down there, just state and federal land. The area was deserted. If I followed them, they'd notice.

But I didn't need to follow them. I'd seen enough.

When I'd been in high school, there was only one reason couples went to the wildlife refuge. I doubted much had changed.

I drove past Ridge Road and headed toward home, letting them go.

On the way, I thought about Jessica and felt bad for her. She'd been betrayed by people she'd trusted.

I let my mind drift and imagined her sitting next to me as I drove, leaning against the passenger window and staring out at nothing.

I thought about what I might've said if she'd been there, but nothing came to me. I would've wanted to help, but I wasn't good at that kind of thing.

Luckily, I didn't have to say anything.

Jessica spoke to me.

"I'm not surprised," she said, her voice clear and calm. "But it's OK. They deserve each other."

The insistence and strength of her voice shocked me.

I pictured her next to me, staring out the window, her face reflected in the glass.

She was smiling, and she was beautiful.

10

The envelope was on the kitchen table. My name was written on the front in handwriting I recognized right away. When I slid my finger under the flap, the envelope tore and something fell out and landed on the table. For a moment I didn't move. Then I reached down and picked up the bracelet.

It was made out of red and blue string, and the colors vibrated off each other like something alive. I squeezed it between my fingers then held it under my nose and inhaled.

Eventually, I unfolded the note and read:

Dexter,
I love you, and I hope you understand.
Elizabeth

I read it twice, then dropped it on the table and walked down the hall to our bedroom. Her closet was empty. All she'd left were a few wire hangers and an empty cardboard box where she'd kept her shoes.

I felt like I'd been robbed.

I grabbed a pair of pants from my drawer and slid them on, then went back to the kitchen and took a few beers from the case I'd bought that morning. I put the rest in the refrigerator then went out to the porch.

The afternoon was calm and warm. I leaned back in my wicker chair and opened one of the beers.

By the time I'd finished the first one and half the second, I was in tears. It was the first time I'd cried since the funeral over a year ago.

Fifteen years with Liz, twelve with Clara. All of it in the same house, overlooking the same field and the same empty road unfurling under a turquoise sky.

I let the tears come.

When I finished my beer, I set the empty bottle on the porch next to my feet, then leaned back and closed my eyes.

Liz still loved me, even told me so in the note. Things could be fixed. I hadn't pushed her away for good. She'd come back if the situation improved and if I started taking my pills.

But I hoped there was another way.

The only other chance I had was finding the person who'd killed Jessica. If I could do that, Liz would see I was a good person and she'd come back, pills or no pills.

The idea made me smile. I got up and walked down the steps and across the lawn to my truck. I kept thinking about how Liz would react if I found Jessica's killer. But not just Liz—everyone in town would know.

I'd be a hero.

I grabbed my whiskey-soaked clothes from the back

of the truck and shook the rest of the broken glass out over the driveway, then took them inside and tossed them in the washing machine. I added soap and turned on the water then went back to the bedroom.

My clothes from the night before were lying in a pile in the corner. They were soaked through, and when I picked them up, water dripped off them and onto the floor.

I held them out in front of me, examining the streaks of mud and trying to make sense of what I was seeing. I'd come inside long before the heavy rain started. I even remembered taking them off before going to bed. They hadn't been wet, and they definitely hadn't been muddy.

I walked back to the laundry room, holding the clothes out in front of me, then dropped them on top of the dryer and spread them out.

There was a lump in the front pocket of the pants. I reached inside, and my hand closed on something cold and metal and round. I took it out and held it in my palm, felt my throat tighten. It was a ring.

There was tape wrapped around the underside of the band. A football and goal posts were embossed on one side, the initials JHS on the other.

Jessica's ring.

11

I walked through the field and crossed the ravine to the cottonwood grove. There was no wind, and the trees were silent and still. I saw the black fabric of Jessica's uniform in the bend of corn beyond the trees, and I squeezed the ring tight in my hand, feeling it dig into my palm.

I stopped at the edge of the grove, looked down at the ring, and traced the embossed goal posts with my finger.

I still couldn't believe it.

I had no memory of taking the ring off her finger and no idea how it'd wound up in my pocket, but it was there just the same. The only explanation I could think of was one I wasn't ready to accept.

I looked at Jessica's body in the corn then moved closer. The rain had been heavy the night before, and the ground around her was soft and damp. If I had been out there last night, any sign had been washed away.

Jessica's uniform was wet and covered with leaves that had been knocked loose off the corn. I crouched next to her and brushed them away, then looked at her right hand. The palm was facing up, but I could see the metal band on her middle finger.

The ring was still there.

I held up the one I'd found in my pocket and examined it again, then reached for her right hand and turned it over.

The ring she had on was a JHS class ring, just like the one I'd found, except this one had a baseball and an American flag embossed on the side.

My ring.

I felt the air rush out of my lungs and tore at the ring on her finger, trying to get it to come off. It was tight, and when I pulled, I felt her skin slide loose over the bone.

When it came off I held the ring up for a better look. I knew every scratch and imperfection. It was definitely my ring.

I sat down hard on the ground next to her body and tried to calm myself. It didn't work.

I had been out the night before. I'd swapped the rings and had no memory of doing it.

I got to my knees and put my ring in my pocket, then took Jessica's hand and tried to slide her ring back on her middle finger. It wouldn't go. Her finger had swollen, and the ring wouldn't slide past the second knuckle.

I felt my heart throb in the back of my throat, and tried to peel the tape off the band. My hands shook and it took a few tries, but eventually the tape came off. When I tried again, the ring slid on easily.

I put her hand back at her side, palm up, then stood

and gathered the tape from the ground and started back toward the grove.

I told myself that no one knew the tape had been there and that everything was going to be OK.

As long as the rings were all there was.

I thought about the night before and tried to remember anything else I might've done, but all I remembered was climbing into bed and going to sleep, nothing more.

I'd never had a blackout so total, and it scared me. In the past I'd always been able to piece together my actions, but this time there was only emptiness.

A skip in my memory.

I passed through the grove and back into the ravine. My tractor was still where I'd left it. I walked over and leaned against it and tried to think.

The idea of going back on my pills didn't seem quite so bad anymore.

I was in over my head, and it was obvious.

I wanted to find the people responsible for Jessica's death, and I wanted to show Liz she could trust me again, but without my pills I wouldn't be able to do either.

I had to stop kidding myself.

I climbed out of the ravine and walked through the break in the cornfield toward home. As I walked, I heard Jessica's voice in my mind. Not strong like before, but just as clear.

"It never used to fit. They'll know."

I stopped walking and looked down at the crumple of tape in my hand, then back toward the grove.

When they found the body, they'd know I'd been out there. I wouldn't be able to hide it anymore, and there was nothing I could do to stop it.

They'd know.

Everyone would know.

The cornfield seemed to spin, and for a moment my vision darkened. I thought I heard someone's footsteps coming down the path in the corn behind me. I turned. There was a shadow, and for a moment I thought I saw—

Nothing.

I closed my eyes and focused on my breathing and the beat of my heart. When I opened them again, everything was back to normal.

I scanned the path and the rows of corn around me. Then, when I was sure I was alone, I turned and kept walking toward home.

12

"Hello, you've reached the Rowe residence. Please leave a message and I'll call you back."

I waited for the beep.

"Liz, call me as soon as you get this. We need to talk about a few things." I spoke slow and tried to sound casual. "Nothing big, just some things I've been thinking about."

I paused, then said, "Mostly I wanted to tell you I'm sorry for the other night. Everything came to the surface and I wasn't myself. You know that's not me, Liz. You know I'd never hurt you, I was just confused and angry, I didn't know what—"

The machine beeped and cut me off.

I held the phone against my ear for a moment then redialed Liz's mother's house. It rang five times before the machine picked up.

"Me again," I said after the beep. "I can tell you all this when you call me back, but if you don't plan on doing that, I need to say one more thing."

I looked up at the kitchen window and saw the afternoon sun reflecting in from the outside world. I heard

Jessica's voice tell me there were other options, that I didn't have to say anything.

I ignored her.

"I'm going to start my medication again."

Jessica's voice faded, and I felt completely alone.

"I know I should start the pills and then tell you, but I wanted you to know right away. Tomorrow I'm going into town to fill my prescription. It's been a while, but I shouldn't have any problems. If I do, I'll have them call Dr. Conner up at Archway. He'll take care of it over the phone."

I crossed to the refrigerator and grabbed a beer. Something moved outside the window, but I didn't look up, didn't want to. Instead, I set the bottle on the table and paced the room while I spoke.

"I want you to know you don't have to be scared of me and you don't have to leave." I paused. "I mean, I'm not saying you should come home tonight or anything, I just—"

The machine beeped and clicked off.

"Shit."

I hung up and redialed and waited for the beep again, then said, "Tell Ellen I'm sorry. I shouldn't leave all of this on her machine, so I'll make this one short. I'd like you to come home when you feel better about us, OK? We can work through this together, and I'm willing to do whatever it takes because I love you."

Jessica's voice came again, stronger this time, bouncing through my mind in a little girl's singsong tone.

"But she doesn't love you."

I sat at the table and picked at the label on the bottle, then took a drink. Jessica's voice was getting louder, closer, repeating over and over.

"But she doesn't love you. She doesn't love you."

I closed my eyes and bit the insides of my cheeks and whispered, "Stop it."

I didn't think I'd said it loud enough for it to come through on the message, but just in case I thought it might be a good idea to hang up. The last thing I wanted was to sound crazy.

"Call me please, Liz," I said. "I lov—"

The machine clicked off.

I let the phone drop. It bounced off my lap, hit the floor, and slid toward the wall, pulled by the cord.

I sat for a while, breathing slow, trying to silence Jessica's voice in my head.

Eventually it faded.

I finished my beer, then took a bottle of Johnny Walker from the cabinet and went outside. I sat on the porch steps and stared out at the field.

I wondered if Liz would return my call.

Part of me didn't think she would.

I sat and drank for a long time. After a while, I eased back on the porch, closed my eyes, and slept.

I didn't dream.

When I woke, the shadows had stretched long toward the east. The wind had picked up, and the cottonwoods in the grove swayed like false gods, holding dominion over their flock.

I looked down at the bottle. It was almost gone, and I considered getting up and grabbing another. Instead, I stayed where I was and closed my eyes again, imagining Liz was there with me.

I pictured her dark hair pulled back and tied into a loose bun just above her neck, the way she'd worn it every summer since we'd met. She was sitting in her chair, her legs tucked under her, a book open on her lap.

"What are you reading?" I asked.

She looked up and smiled, then went back to her book.

Behind her the sunlight dripped soft and golden across the field. I watched her for a while, then said, "You didn't have to leave. We could've worked things out."

She ignored me, but I didn't care. I needed to talk to someone, anyone, real or not.

I stared out at the field and the wide break in the rows further down.

"I think I might've done something really bad," I said. "The night you were here."

No answer.

"I had a blackout. The first one since Tony Quinn."

Liz and I hadn't discussed Tony since before we were married, and I knew if anything would get her attention, it was the mention of his name. But she still didn't look up from her book.

"I think it happened again, but I'm not sure."

Somewhere far off, I heard someone laugh. It was a girl's voice; then it was gone.

I thought about Tony and the night downtown and how the blood had looked black under the streetlight. I remembered the small chip of bone they'd found in my pocket after I'd been arrested, how it'd been perfectly clean and smooth and white. I remember hoping they'd let me keep it, but they didn't.

"I feel like things are spinning away from me again," I felt tears behind my eyes, but I pushed them back. "God, I wish you hadn't left. I wish you'd stayed here with me."

I looked over at Liz, but she'd changed. Her hair hung down over her shoulders, shielding her face. The book was gone and she was staring at her lap, absently tracing the thin gold hem of her black dress with her thumb.

I stared at her. "Where did you get that dress?"

She didn't answer. I asked again.

She looked up and smiled. Her teeth were mossy and gray, and when she spoke her voice sounded thick and wet.

"I thought you'd like it."

I opened my eyes and sat up fast.

I felt the whiskey climb toward my throat and I swallowed hard to keep it down.

"Dexter?"

Jessica's voice.

I closed my eyes and tried to push it out of my head. I couldn't shake the image of Liz in the Riverside Café uniform or the sound of her voice, like she'd been talking through gravel.

"Dexter?"

I heard something shift on the porch to my right, and when I looked up I had to force myself not to cry out. Instead, I jerked away, sliding back across the porch.

"Are you OK?"

I didn't say anything, just stared.

Jessica was sitting in Liz's chair with her elbows on her knees, her chin resting on one upturned palm.

"I didn't mean to scare you."

She smiled, and her skin looked pink and clean and smooth in the afternoon light.

I didn't smile back, and I didn't look away.

"Say something, please," she said.

She was right next to me. I couldn't convince myself she wasn't, even though I knew better.

"Dex, please."

She looked so young, so untouched. Seeing her there drained everything else away. Listening to her speak made the world seem sane.

"What the hell is this?" I asked.

Jessica bit her lower lip. Her eyes moved back and forth between mine. I saw her chest rise and fall with each breath.

"Are you mad?" she asked.

I didn't answer right away. Instead, I turned and stared out at the field, green and gold and endless in the evening light.

Part Two

tuesday

13

"Did you talk to your doctor about this?"

"The prescription should still be good."

The pharmacist typed something into his computer and said, "That's not the problem. You say you stopped taking these pills how long ago?"

I told him.

"Any dizziness or headaches?"

I nodded

"Shakes or tremors?"

"Sure."

He frowned and stepped away from the computer. "You can't just quit taking this medication like that."

"Why not?"

"It's dangerous for one. You're having withdrawal symptoms already, but beyond that, you could do serious damage to your nervous system."

"It doesn't matter now," I said. "I'm going to start them again today."

The pharmacist shook his head. "Mr. McCray, you can't just start them again, either. You need to build to a level that works for you, and you shouldn't do that on your own. Have you talked to your doctor?" He looked back at the computer screen. "Dr. Conner?"

"Not yet."

"I'm afraid I can't fill this prescription without assurance that he is aware of the situation."

"I've been taking these pills for years. I know what works and what doesn't."

He shook his head. "I'm sorry."

"Call him," I said. "He'll tell you."

The pharmacist moved back to the computer and started typing. "I can call his office," he said. "Would you like to wait? It might take a while."

"No," I said. "I'll come back."

The pharmacist nodded then went back to his screen.

I walked out of the store and into the morning.

. . .

"Her mother is absolutely losing her mind."

"Well, what'd you expect?"

The woman behind the counter turned away from the cook's window and shook her head. "Breaks your heart, to be a mother."

The man in the kitchen said something I didn't catch and was gone. The woman grabbed the coffee pot off the burner and made her rounds.

When she got to me, she filled my cup and said, "Couldn't stay away, could you?"

I glanced down at what was left of the omelet. "Best I've ever had, I told you."

She smiled, but there was nothing behind it.

"Megan not working today?"

"She's sick. Told her to stay away."

She started to move on and I said, "Has anyone heard anything? About the other girl?"

She shook her head. "Sheriff Nash was here this morning, asking questions. Said he'd been all over town, but nobody seems to know a thing. I mentioned the boyfriend, said maybe they'd eloped or something, but he said the boyfriend was still around."

"Well, there goes that theory." I sipped my coffee. "Did he have any ideas?"

"If he did, he didn't mention them to me." She shifted the coffee pot from one hand to the other. "I sure hope she's OK. Maybe the boyfriend can tell him something that'll help."

"He hadn't talked to him?"

"Going there after he left here, he said."

I frowned, and the woman must've noticed. "Something wrong?"

"No," I said, cutting into the last of my omelet. "Just thought the boyfriend would've been his first stop."

"Why's that?"

I took a bite. "You always hear whenever someone is murdered the most likely killer is either the boyfriend or the husband, so I figured—"

The woman's mouth seemed to come unhinged, and I stopped talking. At first I didn't know what I'd said, then it came clear.

"Why in the world would you think she's been murdered?"

"I'm just saying—"

"That girl ran off, that's what happened. There's no reason to think anything else." The woman turned away so fast that some coffee splashed out of the pot and hit the floor. She didn't notice.

"I didn't mean anything by it," I said.

"I don't see why people have to jump to the worst so fast." She poured coffee for the couple at the next booth then looked back at me. "There are ten million other possibilities, you know that?"

"Yes ma'am, I do."

She came back to my table. "You watch a lot of those cop shows on TV, don't you?"

"Every chance I get," I lied. The truth was I didn't even own a TV. The last thing I wanted in my house was a twenty-four-hour electronic salesman.

"It shows," she said. "Let me tell you, they ain't real. People don't just wind up dead like that in real life, especially not around here."

"No, you're right." I tried to smile. "I need to lay off those shows."

"Damn right you do." She thumbed through the pocket of her apron, pulled out my bill, and slapped it on the table. "Murdered," she said, and walked away.

I picked up the bill, dropped a ten on the table, and left.

Crossing the parking lot, I cursed myself for being so stupid. I'd come back to see if I could learn more from Megan, but all I'd done was make myself look suspicious.

I sat in my truck for a while, wondering how much damage I'd just done, then started the engine and pulled out of the parking lot.

14

When I got to the pharmacy I went to the back of the store and rang the service bell at the window. The pharmacist was on the phone. When he saw me he raised one finger and continued his conversation.

After he hung up he came over and said, "You have good timing. That was Dr. Conner up at Archway."

"And?"

"He said it was OK to refill the prescription, so that's what I'll do." He paused. "He did give specific dosing instructions, and I can go over those with you when I have it filled."

"How long will that be?"

"Not long," he said. "I'll call your name when it's ready."

While I waited, I paced through the aisles, eventually stopping at the magazine rack. I grabbed the thickest one I saw and flipped through pages that smelled acidic and flowery. I put it back and reached for another.

A collage of makeup and clothing advertisements, meaningless articles about sex and love. Nothing in any of them made sense.

I flipped through the magazine faster, then put it down and tried another. Then another. They were all exactly the same, and the pages blurred.

I heard someone whisper, and turned around.

The kid behind me had pomegranate red hair that spun off his head in ringlets. He had his mother's coat sleeve in his hand and he was whispering to her and staring at me. She looked down at him, then up at me, her eyes wide.

"Good morning, Dex."

Her name was Theresa Hall, and she'd been a year behind me in high school. We'd rarely spoken in those days, even less since then, and I didn't have much to say to her now. I nodded my greeting.

The boy kept staring until she put one hand on the back of his neck and led him around the corner, away from me.

I wondered about his father.

If Theresa was the same kind of girl she'd been in high school, the possibilities were endless.

I was glad she was gone.

I looked down at the magazine in my hand. It was open to a page that showed a close-up of a woman's eyes. There were no words on the page, just those two green eyes.

The pharmacist's voice came over the speaker, calling my name. I closed the magazine, slid it into the rack, and walked back to the window.

The pharmacist watched me approach. When I got there he said, "Are you doing OK?"

I told him I was and reached for the bag.

He pulled it away. "Let's go over Dr. Conner's instructions."

I listened to him run down his list and then held out my hand again.

For a moment the pharmacist didn't move; then he dropped the bag on the counter and said, "You can pay for these back here if you'd like."

I told him I would, and that's what I did.

• • •

I sat in my truck and read the instructions on the label, then opened the bottle and tapped one of the pills into my palm. It was small and red, the size of a ladybug.

I picked it up and dropped it in my mouth, but I didn't swallow. Something held me back.

Was it really what I wanted?

I could still tell what was real and what wasn't, and I did have my tricks. I thought if I didn't fight so hard, if I accepted what came to me, then I could control the voices and live without the pills.

I'd been on medication for so many years, and the idea that the rest of my days depended on these tiny red pills made my chest ache. If I could find another way, I'd take it. I knew it would be hard, but that didn't matter. I wasn't ready to give up.

I rolled down the window and spit the pill out into the dirt. I stared at it, wet and bleeding, and thought about dumping the rest out, too. I didn't. Not yet. It was too soon to make that kind of decision. If I was wrong, if I couldn't control my mind—

I stopped myself. I had to stay positive.

I capped the pill bottle and dropped it on the passenger seat, then started the truck and headed home. As I drove, the idea I wouldn't be able to do it came back, and I started to wonder if I was making a mistake.

I just needed time to think, to sort everything out.

And I wanted to talk to Jessica before I made a decision.

15

When I got home, I headed straight for the grove. As I got closer, I heard Jessica crying. I could see her through the trees, sitting on the edge of the field, her legs tucked into her chest, rocking from side to side. I felt like I was intruding and considered turning back, but I didn't.

When she heard me, she straightened and slid a hand across her cheek. "Hi," she said.

I came up slow. "You OK?"

She nodded, her face hidden behind her hair.

"Megan was sick. I didn't get a chance to talk to her."

"Maybe tomorrow."

I agreed, but I wasn't sure I wanted to go back to the café, at least not anytime soon. I figured it might be good to let things settle down a bit. Then again, maybe not going back would look strange.

There was a lot to think about.

I sat down next to Jessica. When I did, her tears started again. I could see why.

Her body, lying in the corn, looked swollen and blue. Her eyes, milk white and rimmed purple, had come

open and were staring vacantly toward the sky. Most of
the vomit had washed away with the rain, but some had
dried in the sun and stood out in brown streaks along her
face and neck.

I couldn't look away.

"Don't, please," Jessica said. "I can't stand it."

"It's OK."

"OK?" She turned toward me and I saw the lines her
tears had made on her cheeks. "It's not *OK*. It's not *OK*
at all." She motioned toward her body. "How'd you like
to look like this?"

She said something else, but the tears broke through
and I wasn't sure if I'd heard her right.

I hoped I hadn't heard her right.

"There's no reason to be embarrassed," I said.

She looked up, her eyes wet and soft. "So, will you?"

"Will I what?"

"Will you help me get cleaned up?" She ran two fingers under her eyes then wiped them on her dress. "I know
it's dumb, but I don't want you seeing me like this."

"Cleaned up?"

I had heard her right.

"At least wash that stuff off my face." She looked
back again, and her breath hitched in her chest. "Oh,
God."

I wasn't sure what to say.

I never should have moved her body. If they found
out, I could tell them that when I saw her I wasn't sure
she was dead and I'd moved her to check. It was a good
enough excuse.

But if I cleaned her, that would be different.

"It'll look bad," I said. "They'll know I've been out here."

"You don't think they'll know anyway?" She held up her right hand and wiggled her finger. "The ring?"

She was right.

"I just don't think—"

"Please, Dexter." Her voice was soft. "Do this for me."

I glanced down at the body and felt myself start to give in. I think Jessica saw it, too, because when I looked back at her, she was smiling.

· · ·

I found an old three-gallon ice cream bucket in the garage and filled it with soap and water at the kitchen sink. There were sponges in the cabinet above the washing machine, and while the bucket filled, I went in and grabbed a couple.

I stood at the kitchen window, listening to the water climb, and stared out at the grove in the distance. My tractor was still out there, and I wondered again how I was going to get it out. I needed to do it soon. If Greg came by again and saw it, he'd insist on helping. That wasn't an option.

I waited until the bucket was almost full, then dropped the sponges in and carried it toward the back door. I got about halfway when the red plastic handle snapped on one side. I tried to catch it, but there was no chance. The bucket hit the linoleum and water poured across the floor.

I stood and watched.

The phone started to ring.

I picked up the empty bucket and threw it in the sink, then opened the refrigerator for a beer. I took my time opening it and answered the phone on the fifth ring.

"I was about to hang up," Liz said. "You busy?"

"Getting ready to mop the kitchen."

She made a quick amused sound in the back of her throat and said, "Don't tell me you're cleaning?"

She was trying to make a joke, but I didn't think it was funny. I lifted my beer, drank, and then said, "What do you want, Liz?"

"What do I want? I was under the impression you wanted to talk to me. Pretty badly, too."

For a moment I didn't know what she was talking about. Then I remembered the messages and closed my eyes.

"Is everything OK?"

I moved to the window and looked out at the grove and thought about Jessica waiting for me.

"Dexter, are you OK?"

"I'm fine," I said. "I got your note."

"And the bracelet?"

I glanced down at my wrist, didn't say anything.

We were both quiet, then Liz said, "Did you get your pills this morning like you said?"

I felt the anger burn in my chest, but I held it back.

"I did."

"I'm happy to hear that." She paused. "What about the other thing? The blackout. What do you think you—"

"Listen," I said. "This is a bad time. I've got to go."

"You sounded like you needed—"

"Not now."

"OK." Liz paused. "Maybe we can meet somewhere and talk later. How about this weekend?"

I set the bucket under the faucet, squeezed dish soap into the bottom, then turned on the water. The towel on the rack next to the sink had a bright red rooster in the middle with the words *Rise and Shine* below. I pulled it off and dropped it on the floor and moved it around with my foot. The water soaked through immediately.

"You said seeing me wasn't a good idea, remember?"

"We can meet in public."

I picked up the dishtowel and wrung it out over the sink as I spoke. "I can't talk right now."

"You in a hurry to start mopping?"

I didn't say anything. A moment later she continued. "What about this Sunday?"

"What do we have to talk about?"

"This blackout of yours, for one thing."

"I don't have anything to say about that."

Liz sighed. "Then how about our future?"

"What future is that?"

"We're still married, Dexter."

"Right." I thought I knew what was coming. Normally I didn't think I'd be able to say it out loud, but this time the words came easily. "You want a divorce?"

"I didn't say anything about that."

"Seems like the next step to me."

"Is that that you want?"

I took a drink, said, "I've got to go, Liz."

"I'm not saying anything about a divorce."

"I've got to go."

"Dexter?"

I hung up.

The room was silent except for the running water. I reached over and shut it off, then lifted the bucket, cradling it in my arms, and headed for the back door.

I was halfway to the grove when I realized I'd just hung up on Liz. And the best part about it was that I didn't care.

16

The plan was to clean Jessica's face and neck, but once I got going it was hard to stop. When I'd finished, I took the bucket into the field and dumped the water between the rows. She stared at me when I came back, but I couldn't look at her.

"You're embarrassed," she said.

I shook my head. "No, not really."

She came close and nudged my arm. "You are, I can tell."

This time I said nothing.

Jessica laughed, light and brief. "Don't be such a prude. I don't mind. It's not like you've never seen a woman's body before." She paused. "I'm right, aren't I?"

"You're right."

She watched me for a moment, then said, "Good. You had me wondering."

I decided not to tell her about Liz. It didn't feel like the right time. I changed the subject.

"I upset your boss at the café this morning."

Jessica looked up fast. "What did you do?"

I told her about the conversation and the woman's reaction.

"What does she mean people don't get killed around here? It happens all the time. Didn't some little girl on a bike get killed off CR-11 last year?"

I nodded.

"She doesn't know what the hell she's talking about." Jessica walked back toward the body. She got down on her knees and leaned in close, then shook her head. "It looks better, I suppose."

"Considering."

Jessica nodded. "Yeah, considering." She stared at it for another moment, then stood and said, "Did she think Megan would be back tomorrow?"

"I didn't ask. And I think it might be better to stay out of the café for a couple days."

"Why?"

"I think I'm attracting attention."

"You're not," she said. "It just feels that way because you're not good with secrets."

"How do you know that?"

"I can tell."

I shook my head. "Don't you think going in and asking questions three days in a row looks suspicious?"

"So don't ask questions."

"What if Megan's back? Don't we want to find out what's going on with her and your boyfriend?"

"We already know. You said it yourself, when something like this happens, nine out of ten times it's the boyfriend or the husband. Megan was involved somehow."

"She was acting nervous the other day."

"She's always nervous, scared of everything. I bet if you told her what we know, she'd go straight to the sheriff and confess."

"You think so?"

"I know she would," Jessica said. "I just wish I could see the look on her face."

"What if I whispered to her as I was leaving, told her I know what they did and just leave it at that."

Jessica laughed. "That would be perfect."

I looked up at her, and when she looked back, the warmth in her face seeped into me and I couldn't help but smile. It was a gigantic clown grin, and it hurt my cheeks.

"What?" she asked.

"I like having you around," I said. "You make me feel good, better than my pills ever did."

Jessica shook her head. "You don't need those."

"Not anymore."

"You never did."

"That's not true. I used to need them, but you're different than the others. You help—"

"Others?"

I thought about it, then said, "My father, mostly. He was a drunk, and when he got bad I'd stay with Greg or I'd sleep outside or wherever. It didn't matter as long as he couldn't find me. Sometimes he'd come looking for me. Other times I'd just think he was coming for me."

I waited for her to say something, but she just stared, that same gray look on her face.

"I'd hear him yelling, but no one else would. Other

times I'd see him charging at me, screaming. No one else saw a thing."

"And you think that's me?"

"No," I said. "That's my point. You're not the same at all. You make me feel good, better than good. I don't want you to go."

"You don't see him anymore?"

I shook my head. "Not since I started the pills. Before that, I'd have to go up to Archway for shock treatments, and sometimes that would work, but he always came back. It was the pills that finally got rid of him."

"And if you took the pills now?"

"You'd be gone, too, I guess."

Jessica looked away.

"That's why I'm not taking them. I love having—"

Jessica's shoulders shook, and when she looked up there were tears on her cheeks.

I almost said more, but I stopped myself.

I'd said enough.

wednesday

17

The flyers were everywhere.

They were stapled to telephone poles and taped up in shop windows. People stood on street corners and handed them out to anyone who passed by.

The man who handed me one smiled briefly and said, "There's a number at the bottom you can call. We'll be putting together a search party in the next couple days if you'd like to volunteer."

At the top of the flyer was a picture of Jessica. It was a bad picture, probably one of those school portraits no one likes but everyone buys. I wondered how she'd feel knowing that was the photo they'd chosen to post all over town.

I decided not to tell her.

"Count me in," I said.

"Good." The man held out his hand. "Everyone's welcome."

We shook, and then he nodded and turned toward two older women coming up the sidewalk behind me. He repeated his message to them.

I walked on, reading the flyer as I went. It listed Jessica's height and weight and said she was last seen leaving the Riverside Café. There was a number at the bottom along with the words

Please help find our daughter.

Something about the flyer got to me.

It was so unfair.

Her killer was still out there going about his day-to-day life. The idea he could get away with this burned in me. I folded the flyer and slid it into my back pocket, then walked a little faster toward the café.

• • •

When I walked into the café, I knew something had changed. The dining area was empty. No one was behind the counter, and the kitchen radio was off.

I crossed toward the booth I'd sat in for the past two days and slid in. The vinyl moaned under my weight, the sound loud in the silence.

No one came.

After a moment, I got up and went to the counter. I looked through the cook's window but didn't see anyone back there. Finally, I called, "Hello?"

I heard footsteps; then the kitchen doors swung open. Megan stood in the doorway, looking tired and worn.

"Sorry," she said. "I didn't hear you come in."

I smiled at her, happy to see she was working. "Are you open?"

"I don't think so, at least not right now. I'm the only one here."

"Then I'd guess you probably aren't open."

"I guess not." She looked past me, and I followed her gaze to a square black digital clock above the door. "We might open again around noon, but I'm not sure."

"Everything OK, I hope."

She laughed. "I don't know. The sheriff was here when I walked in this morning. After he left, all hell broke lose. Mrs. Colton threw a ketchup bottle at Paul, and if her aim had been on, it might've killed him. It shattered against the wall by his head. Almost looks like she did get him."

"Mrs. Colton? Is she—" I pointed to the counter.

Megan nodded. "She owns the place, her and Paul, he's the cook. They're married." She paused. "For now, at least."

"What do you mean?"

Megan looked back over her shoulder and said, "Mrs. Colton was saying something about Paul and Jessica. I think they were having an affair."

I felt my breath push out of my chest.

"I don't know if it's true or not," Megan said. "The sheriff sure thought it was, though. He told Paul it raised some serious questions."

It took a moment for me to find my voice.

"Is it true?"

Megan shrugged. "The affair? Who knows?"

I remembered the sound of the cook's voice, old and hard, and the images of him and Jessica together came in flashes of skin and sound.

Fast, unrelenting, and vivid.

Thin blue panties.

The air around me went cold, and I sat down hard on

one of the stools in front of the counter. I heard Megan's voice, but it sounded thin, far off.

"Are you OK?"

I didn't answer her.

The idea of telling Megan I'd seen her with Jessica's boyfriend was gone. My chest burned, and all I wanted right then was to get back home and talk to Jessica, make her tell me all of this wasn't true.

"You want something to drink? Some water or something?"

I got up and headed for the door.

When I got outside, I passed a couple kids on bikes spinning doughnuts in the empty gravel parking lot. They watched me as I went by.

As I passed them I realized I was talking to myself and drawing attention, but it didn't matter.

Let them all stare.

I didn't care anymore.

18

By the time I got home, the burning in my chest had dropped to a low ache. I'd convinced myself there was an explanation. The idea of Jessica and Paul Colton was too ridiculous to be true, and I was an idiot for listening to the rumors.

I parked my truck next to the house and went in through the back door. I took a bottle of Johnny Walker from the cabinet above the refrigerator. I needed to clear my head, or to at least give myself a little more time to calm down before I talked to Jessica.

I stood in front of the kitchen window, drinking, and looking out at the cottonwoods rising out of the grove, their leaves rustling nervously in the breeze.

Eventually, I felt myself relax.

I took another drink then capped the bottle and carried it with me, out the door and across the field to the break in the rows.

As I walked, I went over what I wanted to say in my mind. It needed to sound casual. I didn't want to accuse her or attack her, just get to the truth.

I came around the corner and saw my tractor still in the ravine. Again, the knowledge that I was asking for trouble by leaving it out bit at me, but I pushed it away.

I'd take care of it tomorrow.

Today I was going to talk to Jessica. Everything else could wait—

Something in the grove flashed in the sunlight, and I stopped. From where I stood, I couldn't see anything but shadows through the cottonwoods. I stepped closer, squinting against the sun.

It flashed again, and this time I saw what it was.

A man was standing in the grove.

He was carrying what looked like a long knife in one hand, the blade flashing a dull gold in the sun. With the other hand, he was holding the bottom of his T-shirt folded against his chest.

He didn't see me, and for a moment I couldn't move at all.

I watched him walk in a slow circle, first one way, then stopping and coming back, his head down. I tried to see his face, but I was still too far away.

I crouched low and started toward the ravine. The downed stalks were loud and they cracked under my feet.

I cringed with each step.

When I got closer, the man stopped circling and squatted next to Jessica's body. He was facing away from me, but I could see his army khaki pants, cut off at the knees, and a blue number eight on the back of his T-shirt.

I figured that once I got around the trees I'd be able to get a better look at him. I'd see his face, and if he tried to run I'd be able to follow.

I'd heard about killers returning to the scene of their crimes to relive the rush. Was that what was happening here? If so, then why the knife?

Jessica hadn't been stabbed. She hadn't been hurt at all as far as I could tell. There were no marks on her body. She was perfect.

And what about Megan? Where did she fit?

It didn't make sense.

I'd made it halfway around the ravine when the man leaned forward, slid the knife under the front of Jessica's skirt, and lifted.

He ducked lower and looked in.

I stood up and shouted, "What the hell are you doing?"

The man turned toward me. His eyes were wide, and I saw it wasn't a man at all. It was a kid, twelve, maybe thirteen years old, and I recognized him immediately.

Jacob Tolliver.

"What the hell are you doing?"

Jacob let go of his shirt, and several ears of corn fell at his feet. He started to bend to pick them up, then glanced down at the body and backed away.

"Don't move," I said. "Don't you fucking move."

I picked up my pace, but it was too late. Jacob dropped the knife then turned and sprinted through the field toward the hills to the north.

I followed, but I knew right away that I didn't stand a chance of catching him. I didn't have the angle. By the time I got halfway through the field, I saw him cresting the hill and disappearing down the other side.

I stopped and bent forward, bracing my hands against

my thighs. My lungs roared in my chest. Electric black flowers exploded behind my eyes. I dropped to my knees, then turned and collapsed onto my back, staring up at the pale blue sky.

Jacob Tolliver?

I stayed there for a while, letting my breath ease and my heart slow, trying to think of what to do next.

My options seemed limited.

Eventually, I pushed myself up and headed back across the field to the grove. As I got closer I saw Jessica pacing around the corn, her arms folded over her chest.

When she saw me she stopped and stared at me.

We had a lot to talk about.

19

"Where the hell did he come from?"

I motioned toward the north. "He lives on Ezra's property, just over those hills. The whole family is over there. They've got a trailer."

"Ezra?"

I nodded. "Ezra Hays. Been there forever."

That wasn't much of an exaggeration. Ezra was long past eighty, and he'd lived in the same house, working the same land, for as long as I could remember.

The Tollivers were new, came with the spring.

I don't know how they'd met Ezra, but I knew he'd agreed to let them park their trailer on his property in exchange for helping with odd jobs around the farm.

I doubted this was working out for Ezra. Frank Tolliver was a drinker. They'd been on Ezra's property for a little over three months, and Greg had been out to their trailer several times already. He never told me why, but on the two occasions I saw Dorothy Tolliver, she'd had fresh bruises on her face. It wasn't hard to guess.

I thought there were two kids, both boys, but I wasn't sure. The only one I'd met was Jacob. He'd come by once or twice looking for extra work. Normally I would've been impressed—it's not too often you meet a kid who is willing to work hard—but there was something unsettling about Jacob.

At first I thought it was the way he constantly fidgeted, or the way he wouldn't look me in the eye when he spoke. I knew he was just a kid and that was how kids acted, but it was more than that.

Watching Jacob was like watching something dirty.

"Why was he out here?" Jessica asked.

"Supper, it looks like."

The knife he'd dropped turned out to be a rusted lawnmower blade. I assumed he'd been using it to cut the ears away from the stalks.

"Do you think he'll say something?"

I shrugged.

"OK," Jessica said, nodding. She crossed her arms over her chest and went back to pacing along the edge of the grove. "Then we have to get a plan together."

I took the bottle from my pocket and drank.

"Maybe we'll get lucky and he won't tell anyone."

I laughed.

"I'm serious," she said. "Did you see the look on his face when he ran? He was terrified."

I didn't think so.

I'd startled the kid, sure, but I hadn't terrified him. With a father like Frank Tolliver, it would take a lot more than me yelling to terrify him. This I knew firsthand.

"You think he'll tell someone, don't you?"

"Yeah," I said. "I do."

She stopped pacing and sat on the dirt with her knees to her chest, rocking back and forth. "Oh my God."

I took another drink.

"What are we going to do?"

"What can we do? Wait, I guess."

"For him to tell the police?" She shook her head. "No, there has to be something."

I didn't answer. My mind was somewhere else.

She watched me for a moment. "What's wrong with you?"

I looked up. I wanted to tell her what I'd heard, but the words wouldn't come.

"We have a big problem, and you don't seem to care."

"I care."

This time she was quiet.

I could feel her studying me, her eyes searching my face. It was a terrible feeling, like bugs crawling over my skin. I couldn't stand it.

Finally, I told her.

I didn't leave anything out, and I didn't try to make it sound casual. I told her about the sheriff and the ketchup bottle and how Megan had smiled when she'd told me. I told her about how I felt like the air had been kicked out of me, and how I didn't want to believe it, but I had to hear it from her.

When I'd finished, Jessica was silent for a long time, staring past me toward the body in the corn.

Then she smiled.

"I hope she tells the entire town."

"Is it true?"

She looked at me. "Of course it's not true."

I closed my eyes.

"How could you even think—"

"I didn't," I said. "I just needed to hear you say it. I knew, inside, that you wouldn't do that kind of thing, especially with that guy."

"Paul," she said.

I waved the name away. "Doesn't matter."

"No, it doesn't," she said, still smiling. "You want to know what he used to do?"

I wasn't sure I did, but she didn't wait for me to answer.

"He would quote the Bible to me all day; then when he'd pass me in the kitchen, he'd run his hand across my ass and grunt. It was disgusting. He didn't even try to play it off as an accident or anything. He wanted me to know it was intentional."

"Did you say anything?"

"I almost did, once, after he cornered me in the store room and wouldn't let me out. He stood over me, not saying a word, just staring and blocking me every time I tried to get by."

"Jesus."

"I started to cry, and I think he got scared and let me go. When I went out, Mrs. Colton asked me what was wrong and I almost told her."

"But you didn't?"

Jessica shook her head. "I was close."

I thought about her and Paul alone in a storeroom. Then I tried to imagine what he'd look like dead.

Jessica must've seen something on my face because

she slid over next to me and said, "He got what was coming to him."

"It's not enough."

"It doesn't matter. We've got to deal with that kid."

"There's nothing we can do about him," I said. "If he's going to tell someone, he's going to tell someone. We can't stop him."

"They'll take me away."

I took another drink.

Jessica watched me, then said, "You could stop him."

For a moment, I didn't know what she meant; then I looked up and saw it in her eyes.

I shook my head. "No."

"You'll be alone."

"I can't do that."

Jessica didn't say anything else. After a while, she stood up and was gone.

I stayed in the grove, drinking, watching the sun sink toward the horizon. Then I got up and crossed the field toward the hills to the north.

When I got to the top, I looked down and saw the Tollivers' trailer on the other side. It was parked at the end of a gravel path, surrounded by weeds and garbage. Alongside the trailer was a rusted green pickup truck. All four tires were flat, and an engine block sat heavy in the back. The shocks sagged under the weight. There were no other cars around.

I stayed for a while, watching the trailer for movement while the sky burned red.

thursday

20

When I got to town, I drove past the Riverside Café but didn't stop. The lights were off, and there were no cars in the parking lot. I took it as a sign. Jessica might think it was all in my head, but I knew it would look suspicious if I kept showing up every day and asking questions. I'd decided to give it a couple days to cool down.

Then again, if Jacob Tolliver called the police, looking suspicious wouldn't matter anymore.

But I wasn't ready to think about that.

With the café closed, I drove to the grocery store and went inside. Liz had always done the shopping, and I had no idea where to start. In the end, I went for what was easy: frozen dinners, macaroni and cheese, bologna, bread, and so on. I also picked up two bottles of wine and a bottle opener.

When I'd finished, I pushed the cart up to the register and started unloading everything onto the conveyor belt.

The kid behind the register didn't look much older than sixteen or seventeen, and when he saw the wine he shook his head and said, "I'll have to call a manager. I can't sell alcohol."

While he picked up a phone and called for a manager, I reached for one of the gossip papers in the rack by the register and pretended to read about some stranger's affair and impending divorce.

When the manager showed up, the kid stepped aside. The manager ran my wine bottles over the scanner then stared at me for a moment and said, "Dex?"

At first he didn't look familiar, then it came to me.

"Hey. Eddie Sears."

Eddie shook his head. "Goddamn, you've gotten old. How've you been?"

"Been worse," I said.

Eddie laughed. "Haven't we all."

At one time Eddie had been married to a girl named Mindy. She'd been a close friend of Liz's from college, and they'd even come over to our house for dinner a few times when Clara was a baby. Nice couple.

Eddie watched me for a moment then stepped aside and let the kid scan the rest of my groceries. "How's Liz? You two holding up?"

"By a string," I said. "You and Mindy?"

He shook his head. "Afraid not. I managed to drive that marriage into the dirt a long time ago. I take it Liz didn't tell you."

"She might've. I don't keep up."

Maybe Liz had said something about him losing their savings on the craps tables in the casinos across the river, but I wasn't sure and didn't want to say anything in case I was wrong.

We were both quiet for a while, then Eddie said, "Listen, it was good seeing you." He motioned toward the back of the store. "Have to get to work."

"Take care, Ed."

"Tell Liz I said hello, will ya?"

I told him I would, and he disappeared between the aisles. I was never good at small talk, and the entire meeting gave me a sick feeling in the center of my chest.

I wanted to leave.

I thought about Jessica and about the Tolliver kid and wondered if he'd told anyone about her yet. It was a big secret, probably too big for him to keep to himself, and I was sure it would only be a matter of time before it came out.

I felt helpless, knowing there was nothing I could do.

Well, almost nothing.

"That's a lot of macaroni and cheese." The kid finished bagging my groceries and smiled. "You must really like it."

I grunted at him and handed over my credit card. He took it and ran it through.

"I'm the same way." He returned my card. "I'd live off the stuff if I could."

I picked up my bags and muttered, "You're a fucking liar."

I didn't think I'd said it loud enough for him to hear, but I didn't really care. I'd had enough. I wanted to get home.

I walked out the front doors to the parking lot.

When I got to my truck, I set the bags in the front

seat and went around to the driver's side. Someone had stuck one of Jessica's flyers under my windshield wiper. I pulled it out and folded it in half. When I got in, I set it on the seat by the groceries and started the engine.

21

I wasn't surprised when I turned up my driveway and saw Greg's cruiser parked next to the house.

I'd been expecting this.

I stopped halfway, and for a moment the idea of turning around and going back was almost overpowering. If I'd wanted, I could've gone by the bank and cleaned out my savings account. There wasn't much in there, but it would have been enough to get me a long way down the road.

I glanced out toward the grove and wondered if he was out there right now and what I'd say to him when he came back.

It wouldn't matter. He wouldn't believe me.

Again, the desire to turn around and disappear hit me in the center of the chest. I felt myself reach for the gearshift and move the lever to reverse.

I stopped.

I wasn't going to leave her.

I pulled the rest of the way up the driveway and parked next to the cruiser. I opened the door, then reached for the grocery bags next to me. As I got out, I heard Greg's voice.

"Thought you were going to sit there all morning." He was standing on the porch, leaning against the railing, smoking a cigarette. "You surprised to see me?"

"Nope," I said. "Not at all."

He tossed the butt into the driveway and said, "You need some help with those?"

"I got 'em," I said, walking up the steps to the porch. "But you can get the door."

Greg pushed it open and I walked past him into the house.

"You'll be happy to know I didn't go inside."

I set the bags on the kitchen table and said, "Why would I care about that?"

"You mentioned it last time."

I nodded. "Right. When you stole my clip."

"Temporarily confiscated," he said. "Protecting you and the community."

"It's a .22, Greg. How much damage did you think I'd do?"

"You don't think a .22 can do damage?"

I had a feeling I knew where this was going, and the last thing I needed was a lecture on gun safety.

What I wanted was to get this over with.

"Did you come by to return my clip?"

"No, I told you to pick it up at dinner on Saturday, and that still stands. Have you decided if you're coming?"

"You're here to ask me about Saturday?"

"That's right."

For a moment I didn't know what to say.

"You drove out here for that?"

"And to see how you were holding up, yeah."

I started unpacking the groceries onto the table.

"What the hell's so funny?"

"What?"

"Why are you smiling like that?"

I hadn't realized I was, and forced myself to stop.

Greg came up next to me and pawed through the boxes of macaroni and the frozen dinners. He stopped at a bigger box and held it up.

"Fly paper?" He looked around the room. "You got a fly problem?"

I took the box. "You know how it goes."

"That's a big box. Could've just bought a swatter."

I ignored him and kept unpacking.

Greg paced around behind me. "Should I tell Julie to expect you then?"

"I don't know."

"It'll be good for you. Might be nice to be around people for a change."

"I don't know if I'm up for it right now."

Greg was quiet for a moment. When I turned I saw him standing at the sink, staring out the window at the field and the grove in the distance.

"What's wrong?"

"Why didn't you tell me, Dex?"

I felt my stomach lurch back against my spine.

Right then, I almost told him everything. That I'd been afraid he would've thought I killed her, gone crazy that night, when I knew I had nothing to do with her death. About Megan and Jessica's boyfriend and how I was convinced they had something to do with what had happened out there.

But I didn't.

Instead I said, "Tell you what?"

Greg held up a small amber bottle. At first I didn't know what it was.

"You're back on your pills?"

I managed to pull a chair away from the table and sit before my legs gave out on their own.

"Were you embarrassed to tell me?"

I nodded, not sure why.

Greg put the bottle back on the windowsill then sat at the table with me. "You made the right choice. No shame in that."

I nodded again, and both of us were silent for a while. Even if I had been taking those pills, I wouldn't have been embarrassed to tell Greg. We didn't say anything else about it.

Greg looked at his watch and stood. "Got to head out," he said. "I'm going to tell Julie to expect you on Saturday."

"I didn't say I was—"

"Just show up," he said. "It's been too long since you've been over." He paused. "I want you to come."

I looked up at him and nodded. "OK," I said. "I'll be there."

"Good," he said. "It won't be bad, I promise."

I followed him out to the porch.

"Have you tried to get your tractor out of there yet?"

"I'm working on it."

"My offer still stands. If I bring that winch by we'll have it out in a couple minutes."

"Thanks, but I'll manage."

Greg shrugged and walked down the steps toward his cruiser. He stopped halfway and looked out toward the grove. "What's all that about?"

I followed his gaze but I didn't see anything unusual. "What do you mean?"

"All those crows."

I looked again, and at first I still didn't see anything. Then there they were, hundreds of them, black shapes lifting into the air then dropping down again like ash.

How had I not seen them before?

"I wonder what they've found."

I bit down on the insides of my cheeks. "I don't know," I said. "I haven't been out in while. Sort of lost interest."

Greg looked back at me and nodded. "I guess I can understand that. You've had a rough one."

I glanced over at the grove and the crows.

"Those pills helping?" he asked.

I made myself look away. "It takes a while for them to kick in."

"Well, it's a start, right?"

I raised a hand in the air. "I'll see you on Saturday."

Greg waved back, then got in his cruiser and backed down the driveway to the road.

I waited on the porch until he was gone, then hurried inside, grabbed the broom from the kitchen closet, and ran out the back door and through the field to the grove.

Halfway there, I heard Jessica screaming.

22

The crows covered the ground around Jessica's body like a fire. I ran in, swinging the broom and shouting.

They scattered.

I watched as they settled in the field and among the branches of the cottonwoods, encircling us, then looked down at the body. I felt something twinge inside.

She looked the same.

They'd been all over her, but there was no damage.

It didn't make sense.

When I was a kid, I'd once come across a flock of crows tearing apart a small deer that'd been killed on the road beside my farm. I remembered seeing them come away with long red slivers of flesh hanging from their black beaks, one after the other.

They'd eaten through the deer in an afternoon.

But here, no damage at all?

I felt the twinge again, and this time I pushed it out of my mind. We were lucky, that was all.

I heard Jessica come up behind me.

"It could've been a lot worse," I said.

She didn't speak. She moved up slow, and when she saw the body she turned away, hysterical.

I tried to calm her, but nothing I said did any good. In the end, I stood behind her and let her cry. After a while I put my hand against her back.

"They're gone. It's OK now."

She didn't answer.

I looked up and saw the dark shapes in the trees, black eyes staring back. I'd never seen so many birds in one place.

No damage at all?

I turned back to Jessica and said, "What can I do?"

"There's nothing you can do." She spoke through tears. "They'll just come back once you leave."

She was right. Now that they knew she was here, they wouldn't leave. I was surprised they hadn't arrived sooner. Maybe they had.

I looked up at the trees and said, "Then I won't leave. I'll stay out here with you. I'll even sleep out here if you want." I motioned toward the house. "I'll have to go get a few things, but then I'll come back and I'll stay."

She came closer until she was right in front of me, then looked up and said, "You'd stay out here?"

"I would."

"What if someone comes to the house? What if—"

I stopped her. "I won't let anything happen to you," I said. "I'll protect you. I promise."

Jessica stood for a moment, staring into my eyes; then she wrapped her arms around my neck and pressed her lips against mine.

Her skin felt as warm and smooth as I'd imagined.

I didn't want to let go.

23

"Why not?"

"Because it's morbid." Jessica shook her head. "And I don't want it looking down at me all the time."

I laughed.

"It's not funny," Jessica said. "It's sick."

I held the skull in front of me, turning it over in my hands. I'd picked it up at a garage sale a few years ago. At the time, Liz had called it an impulse buy, but it wasn't. I'd bought it for Clara. I'd thought she might like it once Halloween rolled around.

I still think she would have, too.

"He has to have a head," I said. "Otherwise it won't look right."

"OK, but not that."

"What else are we going to use?" I held up the skull, dancing it in front of me. "It's perfect."

"No, Dexter, I'm serious."

I looked back at the skull and frowned. It wasn't even real. I didn't know why she was so upset about a piece of plastic, but I could tell by the tone of her voice that there was no point in arguing.

I dropped the skull on the ground and went back to nailing the crossbeams together.

"So, what else did he say?"

I sighed. I'd gone over my entire conversation with Greg three times so far, and Jessica still didn't believe he didn't know.

I went over it again.

"You don't think he's protecting you, do you?"

"Protecting me?"

She shrugged. "I don't know. You guys are friends. Maybe he's watching out for you."

"Greg's first priority isn't to me, no matter how good of friends we are." I'd brought a few old clothes from the house, and I picked up a faded flannel shirt and slid it over the horizontal beam. "If he knew you were out here, he wouldn't give me, or anyone else, a second thought."

"So, what's he doing?"

"He's not doing anything. He doesn't know."

She looked up at me, and I could tell that possibility wasn't getting through. I thought she was going to say something else, but instead she just turned away and stared out into the field.

I grabbed a pair of blue jeans and wrapped them around the base pole. I had an old brown belt, and used it to bind them up. When I'd finished, I carried the scarecrow to the edge of the grove and leaned it up against one of the trees. I took a step back.

"Just doesn't look right without a head," I said.

Jessica walked over.

"You know, just because that kid hasn't told anyone yet doesn't mean he's not going to."

She was right, but I wasn't ready to think about that so I kept quiet.

"You'd think you'd be smart enough to know that."

The tone of her voice was rough, and at first I wasn't sure I'd heard her right. "Smart enough?"

Jessica put both her hands over her mouth and turned away. "That was terrible," she said. "I'm so sorry."

"That's OK."

"I just—"

She didn't finish and I didn't press.

A moment later she said, "I really think that kid is going to say something."

"Maybe not."

"Yesterday you said you thought he would."

"I might've been wrong. He hasn't told anyone yet, so there's a chance—"

"A chance isn't good enough. We can't have this hanging out there. Why don't you see that?"

"We don't have a choice."

She opened her mouth to speak and I held up a hand, stopping her. I knew what she was going to say.

"I told you, no."

She nodded slow, then said, "You might have to consider the idea that it's our only option."

I shook my head.

Jessica stared at me for a moment then made a dismissive sound in the back of her throat and walked away.

As she left, I called after her. "What are we going to use for a head?"

She didn't answer, just kept walking.

After she was gone I turned back to the scarecrow and frowned. I took the cowboy hat I'd pulled from my closet and set it on top, but it didn't look right so I took it off again.

I went back to the skull, picked it up, and brushed the dirt off. I walked over to the scarecrow and wedged the skull on the post, then put the cowboy hat on top.

Perfect.

I dug a hole a few feet from the body then carried the scarecrow over and slid the base into the ground. I filled the hole and took a few steps back.

The scarecrow rose above the corn, a shadow against the red sky.

I smiled.

24

When I unrolled my sleeping bag, I smelled the dusty warmth of old campfires and thought of Clara and Liz. I tried to remember the last time we'd all been camping. Two summers ago, at least.

"Are you OK?"

Jessica sat on the ground with her legs tucked under her, watching me. The way she looked in the fading light reminded me of Liz.

"I think so," I said. "Just thinking of the last time I slept outside."

She slid her legs out and eased down on her side, turning one palm up to support her head. "How long has it been?"

"A while."

"I used to love camping when I was a little girl," she said. "We'd go to Red Creek and set up along the riverbank. My father would build a fire and we'd cook hamburgers and tell stories." She paused. "The stars were so bright."

"Red Creek." I laughed, more to myself than her.

"There was one spot out there, no one around, just up from the rail bridge. There was an ash tree that—"

"Had been hit by lightning." She smiled. "Funny, we always thought we were the only ones who knew about it."

"My daughter loved that spot."

"Your daughter?"

I nodded. "I haven't told you about her, or my wife."

"No, but I sort of knew. Why didn't you say anything about her?"

"We're separated. It all happened recently. I guess I didn't know what to say or—"

Jessica stopped me. "I meant your daughter. Why haven't you said anything about her?"

I glanced down at my wrist and the blue and red bracelet. My face felt warm, and I couldn't bring myself to look up.

"You don't have to talk about it if you don't want to."

I wasn't sure if I did or not, so I didn't say anything. After a moment, Jessica turned over on her back and stared up at the sky.

"The stars are coming out," she said. "They're so clear out here. It's nice."

I looked up. There was still some light to the west, but the rest of the sky had darkened to a bruised purple. There were no clouds, and several constellations were beginning to burn through.

I moved my sleeping bag alongside Jessica and lay next to her. She inched closer, her skin touching mine.

"I didn't mean to upset you," she said. "Sometimes I open my mouth when I shouldn't."

"You didn't say anything wrong."

"I just want you to know you can talk to me, if you want." She paused. "You're so private."

"That's true."

"Isn't it lonely?"

I didn't know what to say. The question was so direct that I wasn't sure how to answer. So I told her the truth. I told her it was.

Jessica didn't say anything for a while, and we both stared up at the stars. Every now and then a firefly would blink green in the corn, looking for a mate. A few had gotten stuck in the flypaper I'd draped over the stalks that afternoon, but even those still pulsed, light and dark, on and off, never quite giving up hope.

"She died, didn't she?"

I nodded, then realized Jessica couldn't see me and said, "Last summer."

"She was the girl on the bike?"

I nodded again, unable to speak. It didn't matter if Jessica could see me or not. I knew she understood.

Clara had been struck by a car along CR-11. The driver didn't stop, and Clara had lain in a drainage ditch alongside the road for several hours before she died. I don't know if she'd been conscious that entire time or not. The doctors had assured me she hadn't suffered, and most of the time that was a small comfort.

Other times, when I imagined her scared and alone and calling out for me, for anyone, it didn't help at all.

"They never found the driver," I said. "Greg thought

it was someone passing through. They probably just pan-icked and ran."

I waited for Jessica to say something, anything, but she didn't. Instead, she leaned into me and put her head on my chest.

No empty words of comfort or sympathy, just that one human gesture. The need to be close, to touch, to know you're not alone.

It had been so long.

We stayed like that for a while, staring up at the swirl of stars, now bright and deep against the blackening sky. I thought about Clara at Red Creek, running up from the river, her towel wrapped tight around her shoulders, her blond hair pushed behind her ears.

In my mind, she was laughing. Happy and alive—the sunlight shimmering off her skin.

I wasn't sure if I was remembering an actual event or putting it together in my mind. The image was so vivid and beautiful that I didn't really care either way.

"Will your wife come home?"

Jessica's voice pulled me back. Her head was still on my chest, and when I tilted mine down to look at her, she didn't move.

"I don't know. I don't think so."

"Does she want a divorce?"

I thought about my last conversation with Liz. "She says she doesn't, but I don't know if I believe her."

Jessica looked up. "She said she didn't want a divorce?"

I nodded.

Jessica put her head back on my chest and said, "Then she'll be back."

Her voice sounded flat, almost sad, and I thought I understood why.

"I didn't say I wanted her back, even if she does decide to come home."

"You say that now."

"No, she's the one who left. She's the one who ran out on me, on our marriage. That's not easy to forget."

Jessica didn't speak.

"You don't believe me?"

"I'd like to."

I put my hand under her chin and brought her face up so I could see her eyes. "This is what I want. This is where things make sense. Do you understand?"

She nodded.

"I mean it," I said. "Being with you feels right. It feels—"

"Perfect," Jessica said. She rubbed her cheek against my hand then settled again on my chest. "It feels perfect."

I laid back and smiled.

Neither of us said anything else, and after a while we both fell asleep, folded together under a pinwheel of stars.

friday

25

I woke up screaming.

The pain came from everywhere, all at once, and I pushed myself up—fast, clawing at my face and neck.

Red ants.

Hundreds of them.

I felt them in my hair and under my clothes, crawling over my entire body, tiny needles digging into my skin.

I jumped up and shook and ripped at my shirt. When it came off, I beat it against my chest and back, scraping the ants away. I watched several drop to the ground, and when I looked down I didn't believe what I was seeing.

Not hundreds of them, but thousands.

The ground boiled red around me.

I stepped back and felt them scattering along the inside of my thighs. I moaned and fumbled with my belt. When I pulled it open, I slid my pants and underwear down and kicked them off into the corn.

I started picking the ants away, one at a time, pinching them between my fingers and ripping them out of my pubic hair.

How had I not seen them? How had I not noticed?

I looked down at the spot where Jessica and I had slept the night before, and I felt a slow scream build in my chest. I bit down hard, forcing it back.

My sleeping bag was lying next to Jessica's body.

The ants swarmed them both.

I felt my stomach lurch, and fought the urge to turn and run. I wanted to be as far away from that spot as possible. I didn't want to see what I was seeing, but at the same time, I couldn't look away.

Jessica's skin was the color of asphalt.

Her eyes were gone and the skin around the sockets had been eaten away, exposing the bone underneath. Her lips had turned black and split into an agonized grin, and a flood of tiny white maggots spilled from her nose and mouth, turning over and over in the morning sun.

Her abdomen was swollen, and several fingers were missing. I leaned in and looked closer. There were tiny teeth marks on the skin.

They'd been chewed to the bone.

I thought of the rats in the field, and this time I did scream. I couldn't hold it back.

I stumbled away, then turned and ran naked through the grove toward the house. When I got inside I ran to the bathroom and turned the shower to hot, then leaned against the sink and stared into the mirror.

I was crying. The tears ran down my face, leaving clean lines through the dirt.

I saw movement in my hair and leaned over the sink,

slapping at my scalp. Several ants dropped into the white bowl, but I knew there were more. I could feel them.

I stepped back and slammed my head against the mirror. A long crack split the glass in two. My legs dipped, and white light flashed behind my eyes, but I didn't fall.

I held onto the edge of the sink and stared at the ants moving around in the bowl. I felt my stomach clench and my body heaved, again and again.

Nothing came up but acid.

When it finally stopped, I eased down to the floor, crying. I wanted to pray, but I didn't know the words.

I tried anyway.

A moment later I felt something scurry across the bridge of my nose and bury itself in my hair. I moaned and climbed over the edge of the bathtub and into the shower.

The water scalded my skin, but I forced myself to stay under it.

I wanted to burn.

• • •

When I got out of the shower, I wrapped a towel around my waist and went into the kitchen. I took one of the Johnny Walker bottles from the cabinet above the refrigerator, opened it, and drank until my throat and sinuses screamed.

My body shook. I leaned against the counter, waiting for it to pass. For a moment, I thought I was going to be sick again. I could still taste the dirt and stomach acid in my mouth, despite the whiskey. Part of me doubted it would ever go away.

I crossed to the window and reached for my pill bottle above the sink. I popped the cap off and tapped one of the tiny red pills into my palm.

"Dexter?"

I closed my eyes, didn't answer.

"Please don't be mad at me."

I stared at the pill, wanting to raise my hand to my mouth and swallow it, but I couldn't. I heard a lifetime of doctors telling me it would help, and I believed them, just like I always had.

If I took the pills, things would get better. The world would dim, the colors would blend, and I'd drop back and fade to gray.

At that moment, it was exactly what I wanted.

"Dex, look at me."

I turned around, slow. Jessica stood in the doorway. She'd been crying, and her eyes were swollen.

"What about last night?" There were tears on her cheeks. "The way we felt together?"

"That wasn't right," I said, motioning to the field, then to her. "And this isn't right, either."

"Dexter—"

"You're not real."

Jessica stepped closer, and I moved back against the counter.

She stopped, smiled through the tears.

"You know that's not true."

I didn't know what was true anymore, and I told her

so. All I knew was that everything had changed and I needed to get control. "Please, go away."

"I can't do that," she said. "Not anymore."

"Why not?"

Jessica smiled. "What do you mean, why not? Do you think you can tell me to go away and I will?" She snapped her fingers. "Just like that?"

I looked down at the pill in my hand.

"Those won't help you."

"They've always helped before."

Jessica took another step closer. This time there was nowhere for me to go, and I closed my eyes. I felt her come close and her hands touch my face. When she spoke, her breath slid smooth and soft against my skin.

"You saw what's out there." Her voice was calm. "Do you think it'll go away just because you want it to, or because you take a few pills?"

I couldn't speak.

"It won't," she said. "It will still be there tonight and tomorrow, and it will be there whether you take those pills or not."

"I have to take them, I—"

Jessica shushed me, long and slow, and I felt her lips brush against mine, close and sweet. "If you take them, you'll be alone, and I'll be alone. We won't be able to help each other."

"Help each other?"

"Of course," she said. "We're in this together, aren't we?"

I opened my eyes.

Jessica was in front of me, and for a moment I didn't recognize her. Her hair was flat against her scalp, and heavy shadows sagged under her eyes.

There was a bruise forming on her cheek, and tiny red lines spider-webbed off the edges. It made me think of her body lying alone in the grove.

The maggots, the empty sockets, the fingers chewed to the bone.

I closed my eyes and forced the image away. After a moment I said, "I won't sleep out there anymore. I can't."

I thought she'd get upset. I thought she'd cry and try to get me to change my mind, but when I opened my eyes she was smiling.

"I think we're beyond that now, don't you?"

26

The kid bagging my groceries dropped the last of the boxes in the bag, then shook his head and smiled.

"Something funny?" I asked.

"That's just a lot of ant traps." He held my bag out to me. "I'm guessing you bought every last one."

He was wrong.

I'd left the Howard's brand traps on the shelf. They didn't work worth a shit anyway, and I didn't want to waste the money. But the rest, I took.

I reached for the bag. When I did, I noticed him staring at my hand and the galaxy of tiny red bites on my skin. He looked up at my face and neck, then back at my hand. The bites were everywhere, burning and swollen. There was no way to hide them.

"Got a small ant problem," I said, taking the bag. "That's all."

The kid nodded. "I hope these help."

I turned and headed for the door, ignoring the stares from other customers. I'd been so focused on getting the traps that I hadn't noticed the attention I was getting. I hadn't thought I looked that bad.

. . .

I'd parked my truck in the far corner of the lot, and I took my time walking back. My skin felt like it had been stripped off, exposing the meat below. My legs screamed with each step. I couldn't wait to get home and take off my clothes and lie flat on my back in the middle of the living room, not moving, just staring at the ceiling.

When I got to my truck I unlocked the door and set the bag on the seat. I was about to get in when I heard someone call my name.

I recognized the voice and turned.

Liz's smile dropped at once.

"My God, what happened to you?" She pushed her purse up on her shoulder and came toward me, fast. She put a hand against my cheek. "What are these?"

The spot where her hand touched was cool and calm, and for a moment all I could think of was how good it felt.

"You look like you have chicken pox."

"Bug bites," I said. "I fell asleep outside."

Liz lifted the collar of my shirt and looked at my neck. "You're completely swollen."

"I'm fine."

"This is terrible, Dex." She reached for my hands, turning them over in hers. When she got to my left hand, and the wedding ring, she let go and stepped back.

For a moment, neither of us spoke. Then I said, "How are things at your mom's?"

She was still staring at the bites on my skin, her gaze

moving from my arms to my face. I thought about telling her she should see my chest and stomach. That stretch of skin was by far the worst.

Instead I said, "Liz?"

She looked up. "Sorry, what did you say?"

I asked her again.

She shrugged. "Things are OK, but I don't know what I was thinking when I moved in with her. It hasn't been easy to get used to."

I wanted to tell her that it hadn't been easy for either of us, that I didn't have any idea what she'd been thinking when she left, either.

But I didn't. I was too tired and too sore and too damn sick of the same old fights.

I think Liz knew I was holding back. She glanced toward the store, then said, "I was thinking about stopping by this weekend, if you don't mind?"

"You already took all your things."

"I know," she said. "But I wanted to see you. I thought maybe we could talk."

"Jesus, Liz."

"Why not? Do you like things the way they are?"

I leaned against my truck and stared off at the cars passing along the road.

"Because I don't like them at all," she said. "And I think we need to talk about what we want to do."

"Do you want a divorce?"

"Dexter."

"It's an easy question."

She didn't answer right away, just shifted her weight

from one foot to the other, staring at the ground. When she did speak, her voice was quiet.

I didn't hear, and I asked her to say it again.

"I said, I don't think so."

"What does that mean?"

"It means I still love you, but it also means we have things to talk about." She paused. "I can't go back to the way things have been since Clara died. I can't handle missing her and then having to deal with your shifts at the same time. It's too hard."

Shifts. Liz's word.

It was as good a word as any.

"How are you doing with the pills?" she asked. "They helping?"

"I don't want to talk about that."

"Greg was happy to see you're taking them again."

I paused. "When did you talk to him?"

"He came in the store the other day asking about that missing girl." She shook her head. "Did you see they're putting together a search party? They're signing people up over in the park."

This stopped me for a moment. The possibility of a search party worried me, but I tried not to let it show on my face. "Why were you two talking about me?"

"I asked him about you."

"And he volunteered the information?"

"I'm your wife. He thought I'd want to know how you were doing, and he was right."

"You couldn't ask me?"

Liz laughed. "After our last conversation? Sorry, I didn't think you'd tell me the truth."

She was right, of course, but that didn't make it any better. I got in my truck and closed the door.

Liz came up to the window. She reached for me, then stopped and said, "I wish you wouldn't get so mad."

"I'm not mad."

"He means well, Dex. We both do."

I started the engine.

She paused. "Are you going home?"

"That was my plan."

"I won't stop by this weekend, if you don't want. We can talk some other time, when you're ready."

"Probably for the best."

She stood for a moment; then she stepped back and pulled her purse up on her shoulder and said, "I was thinking about signing up for the search party. They're going out tomorrow."

"Where are they looking?"

"I have no idea, but I'd like to help." She looked down at her feet, then back at me. "Do you want to come? We can go together."

I laughed. I couldn't help myself.

"You mean like a date?"

Liz shrugged. "It's something we could do together. You know, small steps."

"It would be just like a picnic," I said, still laughing. "Except we'd be searching for a corpse."

I saw the hurt on Liz's face, and stopped. "I'm sorry," I said.

Liz shook her head and backed up. "No, you're right. It was a dumb idea."

"Liz."

"It's OK." She smiled, but it didn't touch her eyes. "I'm pushing things. You're not ready to talk and maybe I'm not either. We've got time, right?"

I nodded, tried to smile.

Liz came forward. "I'm proud of you for going back on your pills. It means a lot."

The anger I'd felt before flashed, but this time it was weak and easy to ignore. After it was gone, all that was left was guilt. "You don't have to say that."

"I mean it," Liz said. "It was the right thing to do, and I'm proud of you." She touched my cheek before turning away and heading for the store. She'd only made it about twenty feet before she looked back and said, "Take care of those bites. They look terrible."

I watched her walk away, disappearing behind the dark automatic doors. Then I put the truck in gear and pulled out of the parking lot.

As I drove, I thought about the search party and Liz's invitation. The idea of spending a day with her touched something alive in me, and I cursed myself for laughing at the idea.

Small steps. She'd been right.

I turned the truck around and headed downtown, toward the park. Maybe it wasn't too late.

27

Two of the picnic tables under the gazebo were covered with sandwiches, potato salads, pies, cookies, and several other foods I didn't recognize. It'd been a while since I'd eaten, so I grabbed a sandwich and a cookie and sat on the steps leading down to the park.

Behind me, several people stood around another table waiting their turn to sign up for the search party. I tried my best to listen to their conversations while I ate.

No one seemed to care where they'd be searching, just speculating on what they'd find. I didn't hear anyone come out and say Jessica was dead, but the thought must have been in everyone's mind. Why else have a search party unless you're trying to find a body?

Of course, you can't say a thing like that. At least, not with Jessica's parents standing there.

"Coffee, hon?"

I glanced up at the woman in front of me and nodded. She was older and wore a tattered straw gardening hat pushed back on her head. There was something familiar about her, and I tried to place her face.

It didn't come to me.

She handed me a Styrofoam cup filled with black coffee. I chewed fast, swallowed, then said, "Thanks."

"It's not a problem at all," she said. "We appreciate you coming out to help."

I sipped the coffee. It was warm and bitter and good, much better than I'd expected. I started to feel alive.

"Have you signed up yet?"

I shook my head. "Got sidetracked by the food. I will, though."

"Which group were you thinking?"

"Group?"

She nodded. "We've got three going out early tomorrow afternoon. We'd like to cover as much ground as possible."

"Where are they searching?"

She told me. I took another drink of the coffee and smiled. They were all looking down by the river, not close to my farm or the grove.

"I hope we find her," I said.

The woman gave me a half smile and said, "I don't. If we find her, the news will only be bad."

I couldn't argue.

"How is Mrs. McCray? Is she here with you?"

Once again, I tried to remember where I knew her from. It could've been anywhere. Most of the people in town knew me by reputation and that gave them a sense of familiarity. It was possible I didn't know the woman at all.

"Liz is coming later."

The woman smiled. "It's so wonderful to see you two helping out." She put her hand on my shoulder. "It might even be healing."

"Maybe you're right."

The woman squeezed my shoulder and thanked me again, then turned back toward the crowd and continued handing out coffee.

I finished my sandwich and tossed the crusts into the grass for the birds.

. . .

When I got to the front of the line, I saw a framed picture of Jessica on the table next to three sign-up sheets. I stared at the photo, but all I saw were maggots and flies and torn skin. I felt sweat bead on my forehead, and I made myself look away.

"Which group would you like to join?"

The woman behind the table looked exactly like Jessica would've looked if she'd lived another twenty-five years, and for a moment I couldn't speak.

The woman watched me, staring at the red blisters on my skin, trying not to be obvious.

Finally, I found my voice. "All the groups are searching down by the river?"

She said they were. "Jess would sometimes go down to the landing by the Jefferson docks to think and to be alone. It seems like the best place to start."

I looked over the names on the lists and realized Liz hadn't been there to sign up yet. I had no idea which one she'd choose. I shuffled through the pages, feeling the impatience of the people in line behind me.

A cold trail of sweat ran down my back.

"They're all fairly close to each other," the woman said. "It doesn't make—"

"My wife hasn't signed up yet. I don't know which one she'll choose."

"We're only trying to get an idea of how many people we'll have. You can change groups tomorrow if you like."

I nodded, then took a pen from the table and signed my name on the first list. The woman smiled and handed me a button with a picture of Jessica on the front. Again, I couldn't look at the photo.

"We're meeting at the Jefferson docks at one o'clock," she said. "See you then?"

I grunted an acknowledgment and stepped aside.

On the way back, I grabbed another sandwich off the table. The woman passing out coffee watched me do it, and when I looked up at her she smiled and waved.

When I got to my truck, I saw Ezra turn the corner and pull in next to me. He drove a 1966 Plymouth Barracuda that he'd bought brand new the year they'd come out. He only brought it out a few times a year, not to show it off, just to come to town. To him, it was only a car.

I'd tried to tell him on several occasions that the car was unique and worth a lot of money, but he didn't care. He'd smile and act surprised just to be polite, but he had no intention of selling. Eventually, I quit trying.

"Hello, Dex," Ezra said. He closed the Plymouth's door and locked it. "You signing up for this thing?"

I told him I was, then asked, "You?"

"Hell no. I'm too damn old to go hiking around in the woods." He motioned toward the hardware store on the corner. "I got a few repairs to get done, anyway."

"Don't you got someone around to do that kind of thing?" I tried to make my voice sound normal. "In that trailer?"

"Tolliver?" Ezra blew air through his teeth. "I'm better off doing it myself."

"Not working out?"

"Not working at all." He shook his head. "I'm just waiting for the day they pack up and leave. Never should've agreed to let them stay."

"You think they will just leave?"

"They better," he said. "Their sort always does after a while, but we'll have to see."

The idea made me feel light.

"I hope you're right."

Ezra and I talked for a while longer. He asked about Liz and how I was holding up, and I answered as best I could, but all I could think about was waking up one morning and climbing the hills that divided my property from Ezra's, and seeing the trailer gone.

Problem solved.

Ezra held out his hand and we shook. "Good luck with the search," he said. "I hope you find her safe and well."

"Me too."

He headed off toward the hardware store, and I walked around and opened the door to my truck.

When I got in, I looked down at the button in my hand. The picture of Jessica was the same one they'd been using on the flyers.

I stared at it for a moment, then tossed it aside.

28

The phone rang as I walked up the back steps. I hurried through the door and across the kitchen, picking it up on the fifth ring.

"Hello?"

There was no response.

I set the bag on the kitchen table. "Who is this?"

The line clicked dead. I hung the phone back on the cradle.

"Who was it?"

I closed my eyes, tried to ignore her.

"Dex, who was it?"

"No one," I said. "There was no one there."

Jessica made a dismissive noise and crossed the room toward the table. She leaned over and looked inside the bag. "Ant traps?"

"Yep."

"You don't give up, do you?"

I didn't say anything. She rifled through the bag.

"You got enough of them."

"I thought you'd be happy."

"Yeah, very sweet."

She crossed her arms over her chest. The bruising on her cheek had turned dark and now seemed to bleed down her face to her neck.

"Have you thought any more about the Tollivers?" she asked. "Or are we just going to keep riding our luck?"

"Riding our luck seems to be working out."

"For now. But what happens when the sheriff shows up with that kid? What are we going to do then?"

"We'll deal with that when we have to." I moved past her and started unpacking the ant traps. "Don't worry."

I could feel her eyes drilling into the back of my head. I wanted to tell her about the search party and how they were starting out miles away from here, and how we were lucky about that, too. But when I turned around she was gone.

· · ·

I picked up the phone and dialed then listened to it ring. No one answered, and I was about to hang up when Liz's mother, Ellen, picked up. Her voice sounded tired. When I asked how she'd been, she opened up to me.

"Honey, it's been a tough summer," she said. "Did Liz tell you I have to have another operation on these veins? The doctor said I have to have them taken out. I'm not looking forward to that one, believe me."

"I don't blame you."

She went on a bit more about her doctor and how he only hired young nurses who don't look much out of college, then stopped and said, "I'm guessing you called looking for Liz, am I right?"

I told her she was.

"Well, I haven't seen her since this morning, but she'll probably wander in soon. I can have her call you, if you'd like."

"Thanks, but that's not—"

"How are *you* doing, Dexter? I know Liz has been so worried about you lately. Are things bearable?"

For a woman who'd lived her entire life in the country, Ellen had a way of making the world seem elegant.

"I'm hoping things are getting better," I said. "That's why I need to talk to Liz. She hasn't said anything to you, has she?"

She laughed. "Honey, Liz doesn't talk to me about that kind of thing. You know how she is."

Yes, I knew exactly.

"I do wish you two would hurry and put things back together," Ellen said. "I love her, don't get me wrong, but she's difficult at times."

"So am I."

Ellen murmured something then said, "It's been a battle for you, Dexter. Your burden is harder in some ways than anyone else's. Liz always understood."

"Not always."

Ellen was quiet. When she spoke again, her voice was soft. "She is mourning her daughter, too. You should both be more understanding and give each other the space you need."

"She took the space she needed. The choice wasn't mine."

"Well, be that as it may, it wouldn't hurt you to put your feelings aside for a while and let her come back to you on her own, would it?"

"I don't think she knows if she's coming back."

"She'll come back. She needs time."

I didn't know what to say.

After a moment, Ellen said, "I'll have her call you when I see her."

"Maybe just give her a message?" I told her about the search party and how I'd signed up after all. "Will you tell her I'll meet her tomorrow afternoon?"

She said she would, then added, "Do you think that little girl is dead?"

I paused. "Yeah, I guess I do."

She clicked her tongue. "A shame for her parents."

"Will you make sure Liz gets the message?"

"Sure, honey," she said. "I'll tell her."

After I hung up, I gathered the ant traps and started toward the back door. When I turned, I saw Jessica standing in the doorway leading to the hall. She stared at me, said, "There's a search party?"

"Tomorrow afternoon."

"You and your wife are going?"

"Yes."

"Are you going to tell her?"

I shook my head. "No reason to."

"If she moves back, don't you think she'll find out?"

"She's not moving back."

Jessica nodded. "How do you think she's going to react?"

"I told you—"

"I bet she'll be upset," Jessica said. She came closer, letting her arms drop to her sides. "I wonder what she'll think of you after she finds out."

"She's not going to find—"

"Does she still love you?"

"Yes."

"She won't, not after this."

Jessica reached out and slid her hands over my shoulders. Her skin smelled oily and wet.

"You don't know that," I said.

"Really?" Her eyes went wide, the whites a deep red. "So you think she'll be jealous?"

"Jealous?"

She leaned forward and pressed her lips against mine. There was an ammonia smell that burned into my sinuses and made my eyes water. When she pulled away, I gasped for breath.

Jessica ran a thumb along the corner of her mouth.

It came away bloody.

"I'd be jealous if I were her." She looked at her thumb then held it out and pressed it between my lips. Her skin tasted wet and ripe.

She smiled.

"You and I have something special."

saturday

29

If I let go she will fall.

"I can do it, Daddy, let go."

If I let go—

"Daddy, let go."

She's already pulling away from me. I'm holding her back.
If I don't let go she will fall.

"Daddy, please."

I let go.

She doesn't fall.

I watch her pedal faster, cresting the hill.

I do my best to keep up. My muscles ache, the hot air
scorches my lungs, the rapid fire of my heart splits my ribs, and
still she pulls away, becoming smaller and smaller.

"Clara!"

She doesn't turn, doesn't take her eyes off the road.

There is an explosion of sound behind me, like gunfire, and
I turn back.

The road is deserted, a line of dirt dividing a field of endless
green. All of it baking under a chalk white sun.

I look ahead and see Clara in the distance. She's stopped at
the top of the hill. She sees me and waves.

I raise my hand and wave back.

She's yelling something, but I can't hear. Her voice is lost in the wind.

"Stay there!" I yell to her, but my throat feels dry and rough. I cough into my palm. When I look down I see a single red ant in my hand, its antenna twitching.

Again, the sound, loud, insistent.

Someone clapping?

Someone…

Knocking…

I look up at the road.

Clara isn't there anymore. She's gone ahead, vanishing on the other side of the hill.

I feel a flash of panic and start running.

I don't know what's over there.

I don't know where she is.

There is a roar in the distance, like the rumbling of an angry sea. I look up at the empty sky, then across the fields toward the horizon.

No, not thunder.

There is a scarecrow in the field alongside the road. Its face is bleached white.

Bone.

Hollow black eyes.

Knocking…

Watching me, and I can't look away.

The roar is louder, and now I know what it is. A car coming over the hill. It won't see me until it's too late. I have to get out of the road, but I can't move. I'm stuck to this spot, and I can't stop staring.

The eyes.

The car comes over the hill, too fast.
The scarecrow raises its head and its teeth flash.
Smiling.
Knocking…
The car strikes.
Knocking…
The sound continues.
Knocking…
And I open my eyes.

• • •

I stayed in bed, watching the ceiling fan stir the hot air. The knocking came again. This time I sat up and kicked my feet to the floor. The clock on the nightstand flashed 12:00 in a neon green pulse. I leaned forward and rested my head in my hands.

Again, knocking.

Whoever it was, they were persistent.

I tossed the sheet aside, reached for my pants on the floor, and slid them on as I headed for the front door.

I saw a blurred face pressed against the cut stained glass in the door. As I got closer, the face pulled back. The screen clacked shut against the frame.

I opened the front door but kept the screen closed.

The man on the porch was thin and bald and had a beard that wrapped around his chin like a helmet strap. He wore a black T-shirt and blue jeans that looked several sizes too big for him.

He stood at the top of the steps, ready to run at any moment.

I recognized him right away.

"Mr. Tolliver," I said, fighting to keep my voice calm. "What can I do for you?"

As I spoke, his eyes opened then dropped back to two thin slits. "You know me?"

"We haven't met, but I've seen you around." I motioned past him, toward the hills. "Known Ezra my whole life. He mentioned you were helping him up at his place."

Frank Tolliver chewed the inside of his cheek, watching me. "That's right."

"Ezra is a good man."

Frank ignored the comment, said, "My boy has been over here before. Looking for work."

"Yep, he has."

"But you ain't never hired him."

"No extra work," I said. "Small place."

Frank Tolliver nodded and walked toward the edge of the porch, never taking his eyes off me. When he got to the far rail, he stopped and stared out at the field. "Ain't that small a place," he said. "A lot to be done out there."

"Is that why you came by? Get me to hire your boy?"

He pointed to the break in the rows then turned and said, "Looks like your tractor got away from you."

I kept quiet.

Tolliver ran his tongue over his teeth, and his upper lip rolled like a slug. "I think I might've passed it on my way over. Sitting out there in that ditch by those trees, ain't it?"

I pushed the screen door open, hard, and stepped out onto the porch.

Tolliver twitched and glanced over to the stairs.

For a moment, I thought he was going to run, but he didn't. Instead, he backed into the corner of the porch, slid his hands into the pockets of his jeans, and said, "You need to take it easy. Ain't no reason to—"

"Why don't you tell me your business so we can get this over with," I said.

"My business?"

"That's right."

"My business is your business."

I didn't say anything. I'd known what was coming since I saw him standing on the porch. All I had to do was wait.

Tolliver took one hand out of his pocket and held up a small yellow disk. He shook it next to his ear and winked at me. "Looks like you caught one." He smiled then set it on the porch rail.

It was one of the ant traps.

"I thought Jacob was telling tales," he said. "Usually the only thing that comes out of that boy's mouth is bullshit. But he wasn't lying about this, was he?"

I stared at the ant trap, didn't speak.

"I was going to stop by yesterday, but then I saw you out there putting these things on the ground, and I said to myself, 'What the hell is that crazy fucker up to?'" He brushed the underside of his beard with his knuckles then leaned forward, smiling. "You don't care if I call you a crazy fucker, do you?"

I looked up. His smile wavered for a moment; then it was back.

"I didn't think you would. I mean, it's not a secret around town, is it?" He laughed. "Whenever your name is brought up, people always have something to say."

"What do you want?"

Tolliver stepped closer, and I smelled the mix of cheap alcohol and sweat on his skin. "Ezra told me you once beat a man's head to gravy with a crowbar. Is that true?"

Silence.

"Said you were just a kid at the time, still in high school, a baseball star even." He shook his head. "From what I hear, you spent a few years up in Archway, getting—" He held out his arms and vibrated them in the air, then laughed. "I'd ask if it helped, but obviously—"

"What do you want?"

"What do you think he wants?" The voice came from behind me, and I turned around. Jessica was standing in the doorway, leaning against the frame. "He's playing with us because you didn't have the guts to take care of this problem right away. Now we have to deal with this shit."

I turned back to Tolliver.

He fished a bent cigarette out of a crumpled pack of Camel shorts and put it in his mouth. "What I want is to come to an understanding." As he spoke, the cigarette danced on the air. "Nothing too painful."

"An understanding?"

"He wants money," Jessica said. "Christ, why don't you do something?"

"Understand each other," Tolliver said. "Where we both stand." He lit the cigarette and inhaled deep. "You see, it makes no difference to me what a man does, or needs to do, to get by." He tapped his chest with his thumb. "I know the way the world spins under the surface."

I felt Jessica come up behind me, her breath on the back of my neck. "You could take him right now."

Frank Tolliver pointed at me. "What you need to understand is that my understanding isn't free."

"What did I tell you?" Jessica said. "Money."

"Shut up."

My voice was louder than I thought it would be, and Tolliver frowned. "I didn't catch that."

I stepped closer to him. He reached behind his back and took out a long hunting knife. It was serrated on one edge, oiled, sharp. "You might want to rethink whatever it is you're planning."

I stopped, stared at the knife.

His hand shook, and I was pretty sure I could get the knife away from him without too much trouble.

Instead I smiled.

"What about your son? If we come to an understanding, what's to stop him from opening his mouth to someone else?"

"My foot in his ass, that's what."

Tolliver had the knife down at his side, and for a moment neither of us moved. Then I pointed, said, "You can put that away. I'm not planning on doing anything."

He looked at me for a moment, hesitated, then moved the knife around behind him and slid it under his belt. "That's good. Ain't no reason we can't keep it friendly."

Jessica mumbled something behind me.

I ignored her.

"Both my boys will keep their mouths shut. You ain't got to worry about them."

"Both?"

Tolliver shrugged. "One of 'em tells the other, can't be helped."

"Jesus," I said. "Who else knows?"

Tolliver took another drag of his cigarette. "I'm telling you, they won't say a damn word to anyone else." He paused. "You don't believe me?"

I thought of Dorothy Tolliver and her bruises.

"I believe you."

"Good. Then let's discuss the details."

I shook my head. "No."

Frank Tolliver smiled. "You think that's smart?"

"I meant, no, not right now. I got someplace to be. If you want to talk about this, it'll have to be later tonight."

I knew Jessica was behind me.

I could feel her.

"When later?"

I gave him a time.

"You sure you gonna be here?"

I told him I would. "I'm going to the sheriff's house for a while, but I'll be here after."

"What are you going there for?"

"Dinner."

Frank Tolliver didn't seem to understand, so I explained it to him.

"What you got planned right now? Lunch with the mayor?"

He laughed.

"No," I said.

"Coffee with the president?"

I shook my head, letting him laugh. His teeth were stained yellow and black.

I told him about the search party.

He stopped laughing, stared at me.

I nodded.

"Jesus," he said. "You really are a crazy fucker."

30

I was expecting Jessica to yell, to follow me around all morning telling me I was an idiot and wasting my time talking to Tolliver.

But she didn't.

After Tolliver left, I didn't see her at all, which was good. I wasn't in the mood to deal with her. I'd figure out what needed to be done about him, but right now, I needed to get ready to meet Liz.

The idea of spending the afternoon with Liz blocked out everything else. This was my chance to put my marriage back together.

I took a bottle of whiskey from the kitchen and carried it with me to the bathroom. My hands shook, and I took a drink before running the water and getting in the shower. Every once in a while I'd hear a noise in another room, but I wasn't too concerned. If Jessica wanted to talk to me, she knew where I was.

After my shower, I went into the bedroom and sat on the edge of the bed. The clock on the nightstand still flashed 12:00, and judging by the small size of the shadows outside, I figured it was pretty close to right.

I capped the bottle and pulled some clean clothes out of my dresser. We weren't meeting until one o'clock, but I wanted to get there early in case Ellen hadn't told Liz I was coming. Part of me hoped she hadn't said anything just so I could surprise her.

After I dressed, I took one last drink and slid the bottle into the back pocket of my jeans and headed for the door. When I got to the living room, I saw Jessica sitting along the far wall by the window. She was staring out at the field and absently tapping her nails on the chair's wooden armrest.

I stopped at the door. She didn't look up.

"I'll handle him tonight," I said.

Her head was still turned away, and her hair fell across her face.

"Did you hear me?"

She stopped tapping her fingers, said, "You're full of shit."

I started to say something else, to defend myself, but I stopped. If I wanted to get to the docks early, I needed to hurry. I would have to work things out with Jessica later.

"I guess you'll see," I said, then opened the door.

Jessica started tapping the armrest again, but this time the sound was different, louder. I turned and looked back.

The flesh on her fingertips was missing. The sound they made was bone against wood.

31

I parked in the corner of the parking lot where I had a view of the docks. Several people had already gathered on the landing, arranging themselves into their preassigned groups.

I didn't see Liz, but it was still early.

I glanced over at the bottle on the passenger seat, then picked it up and put it in the glove compartment. If I was going to do this, I wanted to do it right. If I was drunk, Liz would know.

Once the bottle was out of sight, I wanted it more than ever.

I considered getting out and heading down to the landing, putting some distance between me and the bottle, but the thought of being in the middle of all those people repulsed me. I wouldn't know what to say.

I decided to mingle from a distance.

I leaned forward, turned on the radio, and flipped around the dial until I found an oldies station. I didn't recognize the song, but it was catchy. I sat back and listened, trying not to think about the bottle calling to me from the glove compartment.

More people were beginning to gather down below. Every now and then I'd see someone I recognized, but most of them were strangers. Liz would've known them, without a doubt. She'd always been the social one, while I made it a point to keep my distance. It was an arrangement that worked well for us over the years.

A white van pulled into the lot and parked a few spaces down.

The words *Riverbank Café* were printed on the side.

I saw Mrs. Colton get out and walk around back and open the rear doors. Then her husband joined her on the other side.

For a moment, I didn't know what to think.

I couldn't imagine why she'd come with *him*. This was a small town. I was sure people must've heard what he'd tried to do to Jessica by now.

I thought about what she'd told me, and anger swelled at the base of my spine, primitive and violent.

I reached for the door handle, but I didn't get out.

Instead, I watched Mrs. Colton hand her husband trays covered with aluminum foil, then point toward the landing down below. She didn't seem angry, and I wondered what he'd said to her. How did he justify something like that? What if he was the one who'd killed Jessica?

Did she know?

What if she'd been a part of it?

Mrs. Colton started toward the stairs leading down to the landing, and Mr. Colton followed. I imagined myself coming up behind him and kicking him square in the back, then watching him fall, headfirst down the sharp stone steps, skin flaying, bones breaking. It was exactly what he deserved.

I squeezed the door handle.

They were almost at the steps. All I had to do was get in behind him and wait until—

Someone knocked on the passenger window.

The sound felt like a blow to the chest, and I jumped back against my chair with a sharp cry.

Greg stood at the window, laughing.

"Jesus Christ." I waited until my heart slowed a bit, then leaned over and unlocked the passenger door. "What the hell's wrong with you?"

Greg took off his hat and slid into the cab, still laughing. "Jumpy today, Dex?"

I glanced back toward the stairs just as the Coltons started down. I frowned, turning back toward Greg, my heart still beating heavy.

"I am now."

"Sorry about that." He looked over at me and stopped smiling. "What the hell happened to you?"

I didn't know what he was talking about.

"Your face," he said.

I moved the rearview mirror so I could see myself. The swelling around the bites was almost gone, but the scabs were still there.

"It looks worse than it is," I said.

"Really? Because it looks pretty damn bad."

I told him about falling asleep outside.

He frowned. "Fell asleep or passed out?"

"What's the difference?"

"If you don't know, then you've got a bigger problem than I thought."

I turned back toward the window. "What the hell is Paul Colton doing here? Isn't he a suspect?"

"A suspect for what?"

"What do you mean, for what?"

"Dex, all we got is a missing girl who more than likely ran away. There's no crime so far."

"Yeah, but if what I've heard is true—"

"What have you heard?"

I didn't say anything.

"Don't listen to talk, Dex. You of all people know how that kind of thing can get out of control."

He was right, I did.

After a while Greg said, "Why aren't you down there with everyone else?"

"Waiting for Liz."

Greg smiled; then it was gone.

"Does she know you're here?"

"Are you asking me if I'm stalking her?"

"I suppose I am."

I couldn't help but laugh. I don't know why I found his honesty funny, but I did.

"No," I said. "I'm not stalking her, but I'm not sure she knows I'm here, either."

I told him about the accidental meeting at the grocery store and her mentioning the search party. I told him how I'd laughed at the idea, then changed my mind and put my name on the list.

"But you didn't tell her?"

"I called, but she wasn't around. I talked to her mother, told her."

"That should be OK."

"We'll see. Ellen forgets things. Chances are this will be a surprise."

"Seems like a strange place to reunite. Why not just meet for lunch somewhere?"

"That's why I laughed at her when she asked me," I said. "But these days I'll take what I can get."

Greg nodded. "Well, I'm happy for you." He opened the door and started to slide out then stopped. "You want to come down with me? Maybe she's already here."

"I would've seen her."

"Come down with me anyway," he said. "I need to get this search started, no matter how big a waste of time it turns out to be."

"Why do you say that?"

Greg shrugged. "They won't find anything."

"How do you know?"

"Just a feeling," he said. "But this kind of thing makes people feel better, less helpless. That's important." He put his hat on and stepped back from the door. "You coming?"

I hesitated.

Greg leaned against the door and said, "You look weird sitting out here, Dex. If Liz shows up, it'll look better if you're not hiding out in your car. Trust me on this one."

I thought about it for a moment, then shut off the engine and got out of the truck. He had a point.

"Good man," Greg said. He walked around and

clapped me on the shoulder. "Let's go join the rest of the world."

"That's pushing it."

We walked across the parking lot to the stairs leading down to the docks. As we went, I scanned the crowd, hoping to see Liz. I didn't, and a hollow feeling started to form inside my chest. I pushed it away.

It was still early.

32

When we got to the bottom of the stairs, Greg held out his hand and said, "Good luck with Liz. I want to hear all about it tonight."

I'd almost forgotten. "Right, dinner tonight."

"You're still coming?"

I nodded. "I'll be there."

We shook, and then he moved off toward the crowd.

I stood for a moment before walking to the edge of the landing and leaning against the rail. In front of me, the Missouri River slid past like soiled silver.

This had been Jessica's favorite spot. I could see why. Take away all the people and it was beautiful.

I turned around and leaned back against the rail, facing the crowd. After a few minutes, I began to regret not bringing the bottle along.

"You looking for your group?"

I turned toward the voice and shook my head. "No," I said. "Looking for my wife."

The man standing there laughed, rattling and fake. "I can't help you there. Mine wanders off, too."

I grunted and looked past him toward a line of tables with red and blue tablecloths and several trays of food. The Coltons were standing behind them, serving.

"My name is Marcus," the man said. "I work with Jessica's dad."

I watched Paul lean close to Mrs. Colton and whisper something. She threw her head back and laughed. The sound was loud and unashamed.

"I remember Jess when she was just a little bitty thing, cute as can be." The man paused. "Are you a friend of the family, too?"

I shook my head, still staring at Paul, still not believing he had the guts to show his face around here, or that these people would let him.

"Sort of," I said. "I know Jessica."

"Is that so?"

The tone of the man's voice had shifted, and I thought it might be best to change the subject.

"Do you see that guy over there? Behind the table?"

The man turned and nodded. "Paul? Sure, he owns the Riverbank Café."

"You hear about what happened between him and Jessica?"

"Oh," the man shifted his weight on his feet and looked past me toward the river. "I don't listen to rumors. Paul is a good man, goes to my church."

I frowned. "Does your church care he tries to fuck his teenage employees?"

"Now wait—"

"Then shows up to help search for them when they

mysteriously go missing? And does it with a straight face?"

Marcus looked from me to the crowd, then waved to someone and said, "Listen, it was nice meeting you."

"You too, Marcus," I said. "Enjoy your day."

He faked a smile and disappeared into the crowd.

No one else stopped to talk to me.

. . .

When they called the groups together, Liz still hadn't shown up. I stayed back, working my way toward the food tables. When I got close, Mrs. Colton saw me and said, "No omelets out here, sorry."

I laughed the best I could. "I suppose that's just my luck these days. I didn't know what I'd do when I saw you'd closed."

She tilted her head and frowned. "We decided to take a couple days vacation." She motioned toward Paul behind her. He was scraping a half-empty tray into a garbage can. "It seems like we never get a chance to break away."

"Well," I said. "I can't fault you for wanting to."

We laughed.

I tasted something bitter in the back of my throat.

"So what do you have here?" I waved a hand over the food. "Anything good?"

Mrs. Colton pointed out a few trays of sandwich meat and macaroni salad and fruit. "You missed the rush, but there are still a few things left."

The last thing I wanted to do was eat their food, but

I reached for a plate anyway and worked my way down the line toward Paul.

Mrs. Colton turned away.

"How are you?" I said, spooning macaroni salad onto my plate.

Paul looked up, nodded.

"You taking part in the search or just providing food?"

"Just the food." He motioned to the crowd, which was dividing itself into three large clusters. "If you're planning on going with them, you better eat fast."

I picked a grape off the tray and tossed it in my mouth. "Don't think I am," I said. "Not much point to any of this that I can see." I stared at him. "You and I both know she's not around here."

Paul wiped his hands on a towel and said, "How would I know that?"

I shrugged and turned back to the food. "Just assuming. I heard you two were close, thought you might've had some insight into where—"

"You thought wrong."

"—she might've gone." There was a knife on the sandwich tray, and I picked it up. "If you two were close, you'd know she wasn't anywhere around here."

Paul reached out and took my plate.

I squeezed the knife.

"Move on, friend," he said.

I stared at him.

"You hear me? I said, move on."

I smiled, leaned close, whispered, "I know what you did to her."

By the time I saw his fist coming, it was too late to do anything but take it. The punch had power behind it, and I felt my legs turn soft under me.

I dropped the knife and staggered back. I didn't fall, but I don't know how I stayed standing.

"You fucking piece of shit." Paul climbed over the table toward me. "You want to say that again?"

I did, badly.

I wanted to say a lot more, but my tongue felt thick behind my teeth. I kept moving backward, trying to find my balance.

By the time he was over the table, several people had moved between us, keeping us apart. Paul spat at me, but it didn't even come close, which made me smile.

"Don't smile at me, you crazy piece of shit."

I couldn't stop.

The guys holding him back tried to calm him down, but it wasn't working.

"Yeah, we all know about you," Paul said. "Keep laughing."

I did; then I felt a hand on my shoulder. It was Greg. He led me away, still smiling.

I walked with him, parting the crowd of people who'd surrounded us. They all stared at me, and right then I realized that no matter what Paul had done, or what any of them had done, I was the monster in town, and there was nothing I could do about it.

"Why don't you head home, Dex? If Liz shows up, I'll tell her you were here."

I could still hear the rumble of tension behind me, and I looked over my shoulder. Paul stomped around the tables, surrounded by several friends. The fact he had friends after what he'd done was almost too much.

Greg pulled me around. "Dex?"

I pointed toward the table. "What about him?"

"Don't worry about him," he said. "I don't know what just happened and I don't really care, but stay clear of him."

"Why don't you arrest him?"

"For what? Throwing a punch at you?"

That wasn't what I'd meant, but I didn't say anything.

"I'm not going to arrest him because I have a feeling you said something that set him off. You probably deserved it."

"That's bullshit. You don't know."

"Yeah?" Greg stopped at the base of the stairs leading up to the parking lot. "What did you say to him?"

We stared at each other for a moment, then I turned and started up the stairs. "Forget it."

"Go home and relax this afternoon. I'll see you later tonight."

"I'm not coming."

"Yeah, you are."

I didn't acknowledge him, just kept climbing the stairs. When I got halfway up, I glanced over my shoulder and saw him moving back toward the crowd.

The excitement was over, and people were reforming into their groups.

I turned and climbed the rest of the way up the stairs, then crossed the parking lot to my truck. I got in and stared out at the river sliding past the docks. Then I started the engine and headed for the exit.

33

I drove across town to Liz's mother's house. When I got there, Liz's car wasn't in the driveway, so I parked in her space. I sat in my truck and tried to figure out why I'd come and what I hoped to accomplish.

The incident at the river had stayed with me. I could still see the looks on people's faces when Greg led me away. These were people who cheated on their wives and beat their kids. People who got drunk and ran children down on the side of the road then drove away.

One of them had even killed Jessica Cammon.

And still, they looked down on *me*.

I took a drink from the bottle then shut off the engine and got out. I headed for the front door, stopping to look in one of the garage windows. Ellen's car wasn't inside, and I wondered if they'd both gone down to the river after all. If they had I was sure someone would fill them in on what'd happened.

The idea stung, but there wasn't anything I could do about it now. I wasn't going back.

I walked up the steps to the front door and rang the

bell. There was no answer so I opened the screen door and knocked.

Still no answer.

I let the screen door slam shut and leaned toward the front window, trying to look in. The room was dark, and nothing moved inside.

I rang the bell again, waited, then went back to my truck and took the bottle off the driver's seat and leaned against the fender and drank.

I told myself that Ellen probably just forgot and didn't give her the message. Liz wouldn't have stood me up. It wasn't even my idea, it was hers. I didn't ask to come along. I was doing it for her.

I kept drinking.

After a while I went back to the front door and ran my hand over the doorjamb, then kicked over all the flowerpots on the deck, looking for a spare key. I didn't find one.

I rang the bell again, waited, rang it again and again. For a moment, I thought I saw the curtain in the front window move.

I tried to convince myself it was just a breeze or a reflection of light on the glass, but I wondered.

I noticed a decorative stone snail, about the size of a baseball, sitting on the edge of the driveway. The eyes were huge with long eyelashes drawn above and below. Doll eyes. It was heavy and ugly and painted green. I passed it from hand to hand as I walked back to my truck.

I stopped halfway then turned around and stared

at the front window for a minute. The curtains never moved, but I still wasn't convinced.

I stepped forward and threw the snail at the window as hard as I could.

It went through easily.

The curtains tore away, and a jagged sheet of glass fell like ice, shattering on the ground.

Somewhere a dog barked.

I got in my truck and headed home.

34

"I knew you'd show up."

Greg came down the steps, beer in one hand, a cigarette in the other. He was dressed in jeans and an orange T-shirt with a faded Denver Broncos logo on the front.

"I told you I would," I said.

He nodded then put the cigarette to his lips and inhaled deep. "That's right, you did." Smoke chopped out of his mouth as he spoke. "You're a man of your word."

"I wouldn't go that far."

Greg dropped the cigarette on the ground and crushed it, then reached into his back pocket and took out the clip to my gun. He held it out to me.

I'd almost forgotten about it, and I hesitated for a moment, unsure whether to take it.

"I told you I'd give it back." Greg waggled the clip in the air. "You want it or not?"

I wasn't sure I did, but I took it anyway.

"Thanks," I said, staring at the clip and the row of gold bullets visible through the side. It felt uncomfortable in my hand, and I couldn't wait to put it down. "Let me throw it in the truck."

Greg nodded, and we both walked down the driveway to where I was parked. I opened the passenger door and put the clip in the glove compartment.

Greg leaned against the side of the truck and picked at the tab on his beer can. "I wanted to talk to you about something," he said. "Before we go inside."

I closed the passenger door and waited.

"Paul Colton," he said.

I bit the inside of my cheek. "What about him?"

"I want you to leave him alone. If you see him on the street, turn around and walk the other way."

"Why?" I smiled. "Does he want to kill *me* now?"

Greg didn't smile back. "I'm serious, Dex."

"I can handle myself."

This time, Greg did smile. Normally this would've sent me into a rage, but even I was able to see the humor in what I'd said.

I could take care of myself as well as anyone off the street, I supposed, but Paul Colton was a lot bigger than me. If he was angry about this afternoon, then Greg was right. It would be better to leave it alone and let him calm down.

"As a favor to me," Greg said. "Can you do that?"

I told him I could, then said, "Will you answer something for me?"

"Shoot."

"Do you think he had something to do with Jessica?"

Greg shook his head. "I don't think so."

"As far as I'm concerned the guy is a piece of shit," I said. "Going after that girl like he did."

Greg smiled. "I don't know how innocent she was in the whole thing. From what I've heard, she pursued him."

"No," I said. "That's not right. He was the one after her."

"How do you know that?"

"Because Jess—"

I started to tell him I'd heard it from Jessica herself, but I stopped at the last minute. Instead, I said, "Just the impression I get from the guy."

Greg stared at me for a moment, then said, "Do you know something about her I don't?"

"No," I said. "But there's something wrong with that guy, you can see that for yourself, can't you?"

"Why are you so interested in him?"

I recognized the look he gave me. He knew something wasn't right, so I did what I had to do.

"I guess the girl reminds me of Clara," I said.

The effect was immediate. Greg's expression changed from suspicion to sadness. He looked down at his beer, then lifted it and drank. I felt a cold flash of guilt, but it went away as fast as it had come.

After a moment, he clapped his hand on my shoulder and squeezed. "Julie and I are happy you decided to come tonight, Dex. It's been a long time."

I agreed, and we started back toward the house.

As we got closer, I smelled the rich warmth coming from the kitchen. It made me think of Liz and Clara and a different life.

. . .

The food was excellent, but that wasn't surprising. Julie was a fantastic cook, always had been, and when we finished I thanked her and got up to help clear the plates.

"Sit, Dexter," she said. "We've got our own personal cleaning crew in this house."

She looked at Marcus and William and motioned them toward the kitchen. Both boys slunk out of their chairs and began picking the dirty dishes off the table.

"Rinse them before you put them in the washer," Greg said. "You hear?"

"We know," Marcus said. "You tell us every time."

Marcus was the older brother. Ten, I think. I knew he was two years younger than Clara, and William was three years younger.

When they'd left the room, I asked Julie.

"Marcus is eleven," she said. "William is ten."

It didn't seem possible. That would mean Clara would've been thirteen, a young woman.

The thought didn't make me sad or bring on a sense of regret. Instead, it showed me a glimpse of my future. I knew I would always have a picture of her in my head and with each passing year, that picture would change. Clara would grow up in my mind.

Thirteen didn't seem real.

I heard the noisy clink of dishes and running water from the kitchen, and looked up. Greg was staring at Julie, shaking his head.

Julie wasn't looking at him.

"How are things progressing with Liz, Dexter?"

Greg sighed and leaned back in his chair. "Julie, come on. Don't start with that kind of thing."

She held up her hands and shrugged. "I want to know. If he doesn't want to talk about it, he doesn't have to. I thought he might like to tell someone, because God knows you two never talk about anything."

Greg shook his head and got up from the table. "You want another beer, Dex?"

I nodded then lifted mine and finished it.

When he was gone, Julie leaned close and put her hand on my arm. "I didn't mean to bring up a bad subject, but I thought you two were working things out." She paused. "I hope I wasn't wrong."

"We were," I said. "We were going to meet at the search party this afternoon, but she stood me up."

Julie frowned. "That doesn't sound like Liz."

"No," I said. "It doesn't. I never spoke to her directly. I told her mother to give her the message."

"There you have it," Julie said. "Obviously Liz didn't get the message, so you can't be mad at her."

"I'm not mad."

"That's good." Julie took her napkin off the table and folded it in her lap. "I hope you're able to patch things up."

I laughed, more to myself than her. "She's probably angry at me, so it won't be any time soon."

"Why is she mad at you?"

"Everyone's mad at me, not just Liz."

"What do you mean?"

I heard Greg in the kitchen, wrestling with one of the boys. It made me think of his father and how he'd do the same with him.

"Tony Quinn," I said.

"No one is mad at you because of that."

"They still see me different," I said.

"That's in your head."

"Do you know who I saw?" I asked. "I ran into Theresa Hall. Do you remember her?"

Julie nodded. "Sure."

"She has a son now, and everyone is happy for her. No one remembers when her parents sent her to Denver to have that other baby. Everyone in town knew back then, but no one cares anymore."

"So what?"

"Eddie Sears manages the grocery store. No one cares that he's a thief and can't stop gambling—"

"Dex, none of that matters—"

"But everyone remembers me," I said. "Me and Tony Quinn, and I can't make them forget." I laughed. "The guy was a goddamn rapist, but that doesn't matter. I'm the monster who killed him. I'm the crazy one who went away."

Julie was quiet.

In the kitchen, one of the boys laughed and I heard Greg growl. The laughter got louder.

"I'm sorry," I said.

"Have you talked to Liz about this?"

"No."

"You should."

"I don't think she'll want to talk to me."

Julie waited for me to continue.

"I went to her mother's house today when she didn't meet me at the River." I was still focused on Greg and the boys in the kitchen, and as I spoke my voice sounded absent and far off. "No one was home, so I wasn't able to get an answer."

Julie stared at me.

"I threw one of those stupid cement lawn ornaments through her window." I shook my head and turned to face her. "You should've seen this thing. It was a dumb looking snail, with a face painted on the front."

"Dexter," Julie said. Her voice was soft.

"You've seen snails. They aren't cute with long eyelashes and rosy cheeks. They're slimy."

"Why did you do that?"

I shrugged. "I don't like to be ignored, I suppose."

I didn't know if that was true or not, but it sounded like a good excuse. The reality was that it just happened. I hadn't been angry or upset. It just seemed like something that needed to be done.

Julie's mouth moved, but no sound came out. Then she whispered, "Jesus, Dexter."

"It wasn't that big of a deal."

"We'll see if Liz agrees with that, won't we?"

"See if Liz agrees with what?" Greg came out of the kitchen. He had two beers, both opened, and handed one to me.

Julie stared at me then shook her head and got up from the table. "Dexter's unique approach to getting her back," she said, then turned toward the kitchen and was gone.

Greg looked at me for a moment, then leaned back and took a drink from his beer.

Both of us were silent for a while. Then Greg said, "How are those pills working?"

"They take a while to kick in."

He nodded. "You're still taking them?"

"Yes."

He nodded, took another drink, said, "You're not going to make me regret giving you back that clip, are you?"

"Probably not."

"Might not be a bad idea for me to hold on to it for you, just until those pills start to kick in."

I shook my head. "I had a bad day, that's all."

He didn't speak, just looked at me.

After a while I couldn't stand it anymore. "I went over to Liz's mother's house after I left the river this afternoon, but they weren't home."

He kept quiet.

"I might've busted out a window."

He frowned. "Did you go inside?"

"No," I said. "I just might've broken a window."

"Might've?"

I took a drink and didn't say anything.

Greg glanced toward the kitchen and his family. He seemed to be somewhere else. After a moment he looked at me and said, "Let's get some air."

When we stood and moved toward the door, I stuck my head in the kitchen and thanked Julie for the meal.

"You're welcome, Dexter," she said. "You make sure to let me know what Liz says, you hear?"

She smiled at me, but it never touched her eyes.

35

I joined Greg on the porch.

He had a cigarette in his mouth and a yellow Bic lighter in his hand. He shook it then scraped a flame out of it and touched it to the cigarette.

"You got another one of those?"

He looked at me. "You don't smoke."

"Thought maybe I'd give it a try."

He hesitated, then handed me the one he'd just lit and took another from a pack on the porch railing and put it to his mouth. "You won't like it."

He was right. Still, I didn't let on.

We both stared out at Greg's front yard. The oak tree was still there, but the tire swing that'd hung from the lower branches when we were kids was long gone.

"Remember when you broke your leg?"

Greg nodded.

"The way the bone stuck out of the skin and all the blood." I took another drag off the cigarette and forced myself not to cough. "How old were we? Thirteen?"

"Younger than that," Greg said. "Probably closer to ten or eleven."

"I guess you're right," I said.

"You remember how you carried me on your back all the way to the Doc Witfield's place for help?"

I laughed. "It was a stupid thing to do. I should've called someone, or run over there and brought someone back to help."

"We were kids. You did what you thought was right."

We were both quiet for a moment, then I said, "You see the way everyone looked at me this afternoon?"

"You made yourself the center of attention."

"It's more than that and you know it."

Greg nodded. "Maybe so."

I took another drag of the cigarette and decided I'd had enough. I flicked it, end over end, into the grass beside the porch.

"I guess you're not going to pick up the habit?"

I shook my head and took a drink of my beer. It didn't kill the taste.

"Nobody's going to forget, will they?" I said. "It's been years since all that happened, and people still see me the same way, no matter what I do or how much time goes by."

"They'll forget," Greg said. "Everything passes."

"I don't think so. Not this."

Neither of us spoke for a while; then Greg said, "Why don't you let me have that clip again. I'll give it back to you in a couple weeks, when you're sure you're feeling better."

"I'm fine," I said. "Today was just a bad day, I told you."

"I still think—"

"Greg," I said. "I'll be fine."

He paused, said, "You didn't go inside?"

"No."

"That would've been breaking and entering," he said. "I couldn't overlook it, you know that, right?"

"Yeah, I know."

"As it stands, you're going to have to pay for the window."

I nodded.

"I'm surprised I haven't heard from Ellen yet."

I was, too, but I didn't say anything. Instead, I finished my beer and set the can on the porch railing and said, "I should be going."

"Already?"

"Probably for the best," I said. "I think I upset Julie."

Greg shrugged, and we both started for my truck. When we got there, I got in and rolled down the window. I held out my hand.

Greg shook it and said, "I'd feel more comfortable if you give it back, just until next week. You can come over for dinner again."

"You shouldn't have taken it in the first place."

I smiled at him, but he didn't smile back.

"Tell Julie thank you again for me, will you?"

He nodded and stepped back from the truck.

I pulled out of the driveway and headed toward home. When I got a fair distance away from Greg's house, I opened the glove compartment and took out the clip.

The metal felt cold and heavy in my hand.

I wondered if Tolliver would be waiting for me when

I got home. I wondered if he'd be sitting on my porch, smiling his gray smile, anxious for me to show up so he could turn the screws on my life.

I looked down at the clip in my hand.

Part of me hoped he would be.

36

When I pulled up to the house, I stayed in the car and waited. All the lights were off, and the dark windows looked deep and endless. There was no movement on the porch, and when I shut off the engine all I heard was the soft shuffling of the cornfields swaying in the night air.

I got out and crossed the driveway to the steps, then up to the front door and inside the house. I didn't remember if I'd told Tolliver when I'd be home, but I wanted to be ready for him when he showed up. I took my .22 from the top drawer of my nightstand and slid the clip into the handle.

It clicked into place.

The weight felt good.

"You got it back?"

I turned and saw Jessica in the doorway. She stood with her hands by her sides, absently clicking her fingertips together. Her hair was down, and her face was hidden in shadow.

I had a feeling I didn't want to see her face, and I looked away. "He gave it to me," I said.

"The sheriff gave it to you?"

"He did."

Jessica giggled. The sound was choked and harsh, like the buzzing of flies.

"Perfect," she said. "That's perfect."

. . .

I sat on the porch and watched the hills to the north, waiting for Tolliver to come out of the corn.

Jessica stood behind me, leaning against the house.

"You should meet him out there. Why would you even listen to what he has to say?"

I had a full bottle of Johnny Walker on my lap.

I lifted it and drank.

"You know he'll come right past the tractor to the path," she said. "You could wait in the grove and when you see him—" She smacked the side of the house with her palm. The sound was like a bone snapping. "—pop him in the back of the head."

"Pop him?"

She didn't say anything, and when I turned around she didn't look at me. She was still leaning against the house, but her head was down and she was examining the palm of her right hand. In the light through the window I saw most of the skin above her wrist was gone. What remained stuck to bone in patches of purple and gray.

It wasn't funny, but for some reason, seeing her standing like that made me smile. "Are you trying to predict your future?"

Jessica looked up slowly and brushed the hair away from her face.

I stopped smiling.

Jessica's right eye was gone. Her left eye was milk white and it rolled in the socket like an undercooked egg. When she opened her mouth to speak, I thought I saw something long and black and insect-like scurry behind her teeth, but I looked away too fast to be sure.

"Maybe you're right," I said. "Maybe I will wait for him out in the field."

I capped the bottle and pushed myself up off the chair. I felt her behind me, but I didn't look back.

"That's the smart way to handle it," she said.

"I'm still going to hear him out. I'll be back."

To emphasize the point, I took my gun out of my waistband and stuck it under the cushion of my chair. It would be there if I needed it later.

I heard Jessica's breathing change, but I still couldn't bring myself to look at her.

"You're making a mistake by waiting," she said. "This isn't going to end the way you want. You need to be man enough to take care of the situation."

"What the hell does that mean?"

I waited, but she didn't answer.

Eventually, I headed for the steps. When I got down to the yard, I heard footsteps coming up the path I'd carved into the field. I stopped just as Frank Tolliver came around the corner.

He wasn't alone.

37

"What the hell is this?" I pointed to the two boys walking behind Tolliver. "You didn't say you were bringing them with you."

Tolliver held up his hands and shrugged. "Couldn't be helped. Said they wanted to make sure I wasn't walking into a wasp's nest coming here by myself."

"A wasp's nest?" I looked at the two boys. I recognized Jacob, but I'd never seen the other one. They stood just behind their father with their arms by their sides. From a distance they looked identical. Same color hair, same dirty white T-shirts, both carrying knives.

"These boys love their old man," Tolliver said, grinning. "It makes you feel all right knowing that."

I was pretty sure their decision to come had more to do with the chance of using those knives on someone rather than to protect their father, but I kept that to myself.

"You're a lucky man, but I don't have anything planned except a conversation and a few drinks."

I held up the bottle of Johnny Walker and saw Tolliver's eyes lock on to it. He bit his lower lip then looked up at me and paused.

"Just the two of us," I said.

He looked at me for a moment longer, then back at the bottle. "You boys head home," he said. "Everything is good around here."

At first, I didn't think they'd go. Then, without a word, they turned and disappeared back into the field, swinging their knives at the stalks as they went.

I shook my head and held the bottle out to Tolliver.

He took it immediately.

"You're raising a couple psychopaths," I said. "Do you know that?"

Tolliver laughed. He uncapped the bottle and took a long drink. When he stopped he wiped his mouth with the back of his hand. "You're the expert, ain't ya?"

He had a point.

I took the bottle from him, and we both climbed the steps to the porch. I didn't see Jessica anywhere, and I felt a cold rush of relief. I knew if I could talk to him without her, the chances of getting out of this without having to kill him went way up. When she wasn't around, things were clearer.

Tolliver stepped past me to the wicker chairs. When he went to sit, I remembered the gun under the cushion, and I held out a hand stopping him.

"Take this one," I said. "That's my chair."

Tolliver shrugged and moved over. I went to my chair and sat down. I could feel the gun through the cushion.

"Why don't you pass that along," Tolliver said, motioning toward the bottle. "Then let's talk details."

I handed him the bottle and watched him drink. I'd never seen anyone drink as fast as Frank Tolliver, and I was happy I'd restocked my supply.

When he pulled the bottle from his mouth, his face was flushed and his lips were wet. He exhaled, loud, and said, "Five hundred a month seems fair to me."

I laughed.

"You're not going to argue about it are you?"

"Might as well ask for a million," I said. "I don't have that kind of money."

"You need to get it."

I shook my head. "Sorry."

"Sorry?" He leaned forward, bracing his arms on his knees. "What the hell does that mean?"

I motioned for the bottle, but he didn't pass it back.

I frowned. "I've got more inside. Don't worry."

He hesitated, then handed me the bottle. It was already half gone.

I took a drink then said, "I didn't have anything to do with that girl out there. I just found her."

Tolliver didn't look like he heard me. He just sat staring at the space between his feet, shaking his head.

"I suppose I could've called when I found her, but I wasn't sure at the time. I had reason to think I might've done something to her." I took a drink and handed him the bottle. "Now I know it wasn't me."

"You still don't want me going to the sheriff."

I shook my head.

Tolliver pointed at me and said, "Then you better come up with something. It don't have to be five hundred a month, but I ain't leaving empty."

He eased back in the chair, and we both stared out at the field and listened to the rhythmic buzz of the cicadas coming from the grove. Neither of us spoke.

After a while, I leaned forward and said, "You know I don't have any money, but I'm willing to let your boys take as much corn from the field as they want, since they do anyway."

Tolliver made a dismissive sound and looked away, shaking his head.

I went on.

"And I suppose you can come by and sit and drink out here with me whenever you want. I've always got a bottle or two in the house."

Tolliver, still shaking his head, looked down at the bottle in his hands. "God damn," he said. "Fucking luck, ain't it?"

"It's all I got to offer," I said.

I got up and went inside for another bottle and ended up grabbing two. When I came outside, Tolliver was resting his feet on the porch railing.

I sat down and handed him one of the unopened bottles of Johnny Walker. When he saw it, I could tell he was trying not to smile.

He lifted the open bottle and finished what was left. When he was done, he stood and threw it off the porch into the cornfield.

It spun, end over end, disappearing into darkness.

Tolliver put his hands on his waist and stretched back. I could hear his bones pop.

Pop him.

"So we got a deal?" I asked.

Tolliver glanced over at me, then shook his head again and sat down. "You gonna be here every time I come by?"

"Every time."

He seemed to think about this, then said, "I god-damn guess we have a deal. Your secret is safe."

He wouldn't look at me and I knew he was lying, but I didn't let on. Instead, I held up my bottle and Tolliver held up his, and we toasted our deal.

38

For the next couple hours, Tolliver talked about nothing, only stopping long enough to drink and take an occasional breath. The bottle I'd given him was nearly half-empty, and his voice was wet and slurred.

"Almost a full year," he said. "I saw my share of death, too. It wasn't just a few months of volleyball in the desert like you hear. There was some fucked up shit happening over there, too."

I scanned the cornfield, looking for Jessica in the shadows. I didn't see her.

"You ever seen a dead body?" Tolliver asked, then closed his eyes and put his head down. He whispered to himself and laughed. "What the fuck am I saying?" He motioned toward the grove, now only a shadow in the darkness. "Besides that one, I mean."

"Yeah," I said. "I have."

"The one you killed, right?"

I nodded. "There was another."

Tolliver leaned toward me in his chair. "Is it true? You really used a crowbar?"

"A tire iron."

He repeated the words and leaned back. "God damn, what was that like? Must've been a rush, ending a guy's life like that."

I didn't say anything.

Tolliver waited, then said, "So, was it?"

I lifted my bottle and drank. "I don't remember."

"Bullshit. You don't forget something like that."

"No," I said. "I don't remember. I never remembered, even after I did it. I'd blacked out."

"Blacked out?" He frowned. "You telling me there's nothing there at all?"

"Nothing."

"Did you know the guy?"

I shook my head. "Not really."

"Why'd you do it, then?"

That was the question everyone asked when I'd woken up at the police station. They'd asked it for years at Archway, too. I never told anyone, not even Greg. I'd made a promise to Liz, but right then that promise didn't seem to matter anymore.

"He hurt someone I cared about," I said. "And I wanted to hurt him back, so I waited for him. I wasn't going to kill him, but that's what happened. Next thing I remember, I'm in the police station and I've got dried blood on my clothes and in my hair and a piece of his skull in my pocket."

"A piece of his skull?"

I nodded and held up two fingers about an inch apart. "I must've picked it up after. I don't remember."

Tolliver stared at me for a while then shook his head. "At least you got off."

"Got off?"

"No jail."

I thought about my room at Archway and the electroshock treatments that always ended in convulsions and vomiting and the smell of rotted lemons in the air.

"Yeah," I said. "No jail."

I took a drink.

"You still get them blackouts?"

I nodded.

"What starts 'em?"

"Drinking," I said. "The medication helps. As long as I take my pills I'm OK."

"You taking your pills?"

"Nope."

I lifted the bottle to my lips.

For the first time all night, Tolliver stopped talking, and the only sound I could hear was the low shuffle of the wind passing through the corn.

I let some time go by, then looked over at Tolliver. The porch was dark except for a soft yellow light leaking from the living room window. It didn't do much, but it was enough for me to see his head nod and dip.

"You OK?" I asked.

Tolliver's head snapped up. He grunted and lifted the bottle to his lips. It was empty, but he didn't seem to notice. "God damn right I'm OK."

He was either going to pass out on my porch or somewhere in the field on his way home. I preferred the field, but I knew if he stayed much longer I'd find him out here tomorrow morning.

"Why don't you head home? It's late and—"

I stopped.

Something moved in the shadow behind Tolliver's head. When I looked, I saw Jessica in the corner. She was standing behind Tolliver, staring at the back of his head, not moving.

When she saw me looking at her, her mouth opened like a wound.

The scream was out before I could stop myself.

Tolliver jumped. He knocked over the wicker chair then stumbled against the house, his head twisting from side to side. "What the fuck is wrong with you?"

My pants felt wet, and I looked down at the growing stain on my crotch. I couldn't stop it. I stood and braced myself on the porch rail. Everything spun. I leaned over and vomited into the yard.

"What the hell did you yell like that for?" Tolliver asked. "What's wrong with you?"

I forced myself to turn and look.

She was still there. She took a step forward and said, "This is your chance. Don't fuck it up."

I turned and spit into the yard.

"If he leaves here tonight, tomorrow he'll tell everyone. He thinks there's a reward."

"There's no reward," I said.

"A reward for what?" Tolliver said. "What the fuck are you talking about?"

"He believes there will be," Jessica said. "You can't trust him to keep quiet."

I knew she was right. I couldn't trust him.

"You have to kill him."

I wiped my mouth with my hand and it came away bloody.

"Do you hear me, Dexter?"

Jessica's voice had changed. It sounded deeper and dirtier, like a voice shredded through constant screaming, familiar, like my father's voice.

"I need to get out of here," I said. "Walk."

"Walk?" Tolliver looked down at the empty bottle in his hand, his eyes already reverting to heavy. He shook his head. "I don't think so."

"You can't stay here. I know a shortcut. I'll walk with you."

Tolliver pointed at me with the empty bottle. "You're already backing out on me, you son of a bitch. This ain't what we agreed on."

"I'm not backing out on anything."

"The hell you ain't," he said, raising his voice. "If that's your choice, then that's the way we'll play it."

I held up my hands to calm him, but he wouldn't stop yelling. Finally I went inside and took another bottle from the cabinet. He was still yelling when I got back to the porch, but he stopped when I handed him the bottle.

"You can come back tomorrow," I said. "I'm not backing out. I just need sleep."

He held the bottle up to the light, uncapped it, and drank.

I heard the rumble and whine of Jessica's breathing in the corner. I needed to get away.

"I'll walk you back," I said. "I know a shortcut."

Tolliver shook his head. "I want to see her again."

At first I didn't know what he meant, then it came to me. "No, I don't think so."

"I want to see her and all the crazy bug trap shit you got out there." He held up the bottle. "Then I'll go home."

"It's perfect out there," Jessica said. Her voice was a whisper, but it burned into my head. "You won't get another chance."

"OK," I said. "I'll show you."

Tolliver nodded and started down the steps and across the yard toward the break in the rows.

Once his back was turned, I bent down and took the gun from under the cushion where I'd been sitting and slid it into the back of my pants.

"We're almost done, Dexter," Jessica said.

I held the railing and went down the steps to the yard, not looking back. I felt her behind me, and I waited for her to say something else, but she didn't.

Up ahead, I heard Tolliver stumbling along the path, cursing and yelling.

When I got to the edge of the field, I stopped and looked back. Jessica stood at the top of the porch stairs, silhouetted by the empty yellow glow from the window.

I watched her for a moment, then turned and followed Frank Tolliver into the corn.

39

Tolliver wouldn't stop screaming.

"You're not dead," I said. "Keep your voice down."

"Is this blood?"

The moon was out and there was just enough light.

"It's mud," I said. "You're fine."

Tolliver pushed himself up in the ravine. His legs shook for a moment then seemed to steady. When they did, he checked his bottle to make sure it wasn't broken, then pointed up to me standing on the edge. "I could sue your ass, you know that?"

The idea made me laugh.

"Laugh all you want, goddamn it, but I could."

He started to climb out on the other side. I watched him struggle, thinking this might be the best place to do it. He was already in a ditch. It would just be a matter of covering him up.

I reached back for the gun, but something stopped me. I wanted to see Jessica, but more than that, I wanted someone else to see her. I wanted to see her through new eyes.

I waited until Tolliver cleared the other side, then made my way through the ravine. Halfway down, I stumbled but didn't fall.

Tolliver laughed.

"Ain't so funny now is it, you crazy fucker?"

I ignored him and climbed out.

We headed through the cottonwoods toward the bend. When we came out of the trees, Tolliver stopped and covered his mouth with his hand.

"Lord Jesus," he said. "She's ripe tonight."

Jessica's body was covered in shadow, and as I got closer I heard a low rustling sound. Her body looked like it was vibrating.

I thought of the ants and stopped.

Tolliver came up next to me, still holding his nose and mouth, and when he spoke his voice sounded thin and tinny.

"What the hell is that?" He pointed to the scarecrow standing half out of the corn. "You put that up?"

I nodded.

Tolliver stood for a moment, silent, staring at the scarecrow. "Where'd you get the skull?"

"It's not real."

"OK," he said. "But that don't make you any less of a goddamn freak for using it, does it?"

I didn't answer.

Tolliver looked down and began to circle the body. He leaned in closer and said, "The rats have been at her."

I grunted, watching him, then reached for the gun behind my back and held it down by my side.

Tolliver stopped moving and looked around. "Man, what the hell goes through your mind?"

He didn't wait for me to answer.

He squinted at something in the corn and said, "What is *that*?"

I looked where he was pointing.

The strips of flypaper I'd hung the day before dangled from the bent stalks like swollen black fruit.

"Are those flies?"

He started toward them and stopped. Something on the ground caught his attention. He bent down and picked up a muddy piece of cloth, pinching it between two fingers.

I knew what it was immediately.

It was the underwear I'd kicked off the morning of the ants.

It took Tolliver a moment to realize what he'd found. When he did, he looked up at me. Something in his eyes had changed.

"Oh, Christ, man," he said.

I shook my head. I wanted to tell him it wasn't what it looked like, but I knew anything I said wouldn't matter.

Tolliver dropped the underwear and backed away, into the corn.

"You got the wrong idea," I said.

His eyes never left me, and he never stopped moving.

"Did you hear me?"

No answer.

I lifted the gun and pointed it at him.

He saw the gun and stopped.

"I said you got the wrong idea."

Tolliver nodded. "OK, man."

For a moment, we both stood there. I felt the trigger under my finger. All I had to do was squeeze.

"You gonna kill me?"

I nodded. "No choice."

"You don't have to," Tolliver said. "We still have our deal."

"Sorry," I said, then closed my eyes and squeezed the trigger. It didn't fire.

I opened my eyes and looked at the gun.

The safety was on.

I pushed it off, but it was too late. Tolliver was gone, running through the field.

I saw the tops of the corn shake as he ran, and I pointed the gun in that direction, but this time I couldn't pull the trigger. Something inside wouldn't let me do it.

"What the hell is wrong with you?"

The voice was loud in my head. I pressed my hands against my ears.

It didn't help.

"You're letting him get away?"

I turned and saw Jessica sitting in the shadow by the body. Her legs were tucked under her. As she spoke, she dragged herself forward with her arms, then stood and came toward me fast.

I stepped back—I didn't mean to, but I couldn't help myself. She stopped inches away from my face. Her one milk-white eye rolled furiously in the hollow black socket.

The smell of her breath was horrible. I felt my stomach twist and my throat lurch.

"Don't fuck this up, Dexter," she said. "Go after him. Now."

I stared at her, unable to look away.

When I didn't move, Jessica's face contorted in rage and her voice exploded in my head.

No words, no screams, just pure sound.

I don't know how long I ran through the field, but when I stopped I was out of breath and my chest ached. There were tears on my face, and flashes of white blossomed behind my eyes. I dropped to my knees and tried to catch my breath.

I could still hear Jessica screaming at me to get up, to find him, to put an end to all of this tonight.

But I couldn't move.

I didn't know where he was or where I was. The hills were out there somewhere, my house was out there somewhere, but I couldn't tell where.

I pushed myself up, but my legs wouldn't hold and I fell back into the corn, moaning and coughing. Above me, the stars spun against the black sky, pulling me along.

"I fucked up," I said. "I really fucked up."

There was no argument in my mind, and when I closed my eyes, sleep came almost at once.

I gave in without a fight.

40

I awoke to sirens.

The sound was getting louder, coming closer.

The stars were still out, and a dim orange glow crept across the sky from the north. I sat up. My mouth felt dry and my throat burned. I tried to gauge how long I'd been out, but there was no way to tell.

I rested my head against my knees and tried to find the strength to stand. A moment later I felt my stomach roll, and I leaned over and threw up into the dirt, again and again. When it finally stopped, I wiped my mouth with the back of my hand. It came away wet and dark. *Blood.*

I wiped my hand on my pants and tried to clear my head. When I felt things drift into focus, I pushed myself up and looked around. I stood in the middle of the field. To the east, I could see my house, and the hills leading to Tolliver's trailer to the north.

The sirens and the orange light came from behind those hills.

There was an acidic coppery taste in my throat. I swallowed hard and started walking north. Halfway up the hill, my stomach cramped again, and I leaned over and threw up more blood.

I wanted to sit, but I made myself keep climbing.

When I got to the top, I looked down at the spot where Tolliver's trailer had been parked. It was an inferno. The fire engulfed everything. I could feel the heat from where I stood.

There were two fire trucks and several men moving between them, carrying hoses, pointing, shouting.

Another set of lights appeared in the distance, and then Greg's cruiser pulled in next to the trucks. He got out and crossed toward one of the firefighters, who met him halfway. They talked for a minute, then Greg went back to his cruiser and leaned against the hood, waiting.

There were no hydrants out there, so the hoses were hooked to the trucks. Within minutes, two heavy streams of water had covered the blazing trailer. It didn't seem to have much of an effect right away, but eventually the fire seemed to get smaller and smaller.

I saw enough of the trailer in the glare of the headlights to know there was nothing left. I looked around for the Tollivers, but I didn't see them.

I felt a small twinge in the back of my mind.

Had I blacked out, again?

I looked down at my hands. They were caked with dirt.

I pushed the thought away.

Already the sky to the east had split pink along the horizon. Soon, it would be morning.

I needed to get away.

When I turned, Jessica was standing behind me. She looked past me to the fire, her arms across her chest. The glow shone against her skin.

I had to look away.

We stood for a while, and I listened to the cold rattle of her breathing. When she turned away from the fire she made one lurching step toward me, stopping with her face next to mine.

I stared at the ground.

"You did this?"

I shook my head. "No, I didn't."

She turned her head toward the fire, and several maggots dropped at her feet. They twisted, fat and orange in the light.

I stepped back. The urge to throw up was overpowering, but I knew if I did I wouldn't be able to stop. I fought to keep it down.

"You did this."

It wasn't a question this time. I kept my mouth shut. Jessica turned back to me, and I saw the skin on her face stretch and split along her cheeks.

She was smiling.

"Maybe you're not completely useless after all," she said, then stepped closer and took a deep, wet breath. She exhaled against my skin, blowing my hair away from my forehead. "But I guess we'll see, won't we?"

The smell of her breath made my eyes water, and a small cry slipped from somewhere deep in my throat.

Jessica heard it and laughed.

She stared at me for a moment longer, still smiling, then turned and walked down the hill and disappeared into the grove.

Part Three

sunday

41

When I looked down, there was blood in the sink, dark and thick. I coughed, spat, then ran the water and watched it all circle into the drain.

Once the blood was gone, I washed my face and waited to see if the sickness would return. It didn't. I shut off the water and walked slowly toward the kitchen.

My pills were sitting on the windowsill.

I set the gun on the sink then opened the bottle and slid one of the tiny red pills into my mouth and swallowed it dry.

No hesitation. No indecision. Only faith things would get better.

"Oh, Dexter," Jessica's voice sounded flat. "You know it's much too late for that."

I bit down on the inside of my cheeks. "Shut up."

Jessica giggled. The sound was insanity.

I slid my gun into the back of my pants and walked out through the front door and down the driveway to the road.

I wanted to go to Ezra's and see what was left of Tolliver's trailer, but I couldn't bring myself to pass through the field again. The road would take longer, but I didn't care.

When I got to Ezra's, I kept walking until I came to the spot where Tolliver had been parked. Ezra was there, standing outside the burnt ruins of the trailer. His back was turned, and I called out to him as I got close. He looked at me briefly, nodded, then turned back to the twist of black metal and ash.

"The boys weren't even supposed to be inside," he said. "Mrs. Tolliver had planned on taking them up to Des Moines yesterday." He shook his head. "God damn luck of it."

"Were they all inside?"

Ezra nodded. "Fire department said the smoke probably got 'em before the fire, but that don't mean too much. I still feel for those boys."

I agreed it was a shame, then kept quiet.

The air had a heavy chemical smell to it. I looked down and kicked a charred piece of wood toward the blackened trailer frame, then said, "They say anything else?"

"Who?"

"The fire department?"

Ezra shook his head. "Not to me. Saw 'em talking to Nash for a long while. Probably making sure they're both on the same page for the investigation."

"They say how it started?"

"That's what they're investigating." He wore a green John Deere baseball cap, and he took it off and wiped his forehead on his sleeve. "Did I tell you they were stealing from me?"

"No," I said. "Stealing what?"

"Don't know how long it'd been going on, but I got a call yesterday from Charley Ulrich over at the Pawn & Loan. He called to say Frank was in there with a World War Two Bronze Star. Said he asked him where he came by that medal, and Frank told him it'd belonged to his grandfather." Ezra slid the John Deere cap back on his head. "Can you believe that?"

I could believe it, but I kept quiet.

"Charley knew I was the only one in town with a Bronze Star, so he went into the back and called me and asked if mine had gone missing. I went to check, and sure enough, the case was empty. Son of a bitch took it right out of the top drawer in my bedroom."

"You get it back?"

"Damn right I did. Charley said he was going to call Sheriff Nash, but Frank must've got suspicious because he was gone by the time Charley came out."

"Did you confront him?"

"Came by yesterday to tell him to get off my god-damn property, but no one was out here. I remembered Dorothy saying she was taking the boys out of town for a few days, but I knew Frank was around. Off drunk somewhere, more than likely."

"Better to let Greg handle him anyway."

Ezra stared at what was left of the trailer, but his eyes looked distant, unfocused. I wasn't sure he'd heard me, and I started to repeat myself; then he spoke.

"Hate to see 'em dead, but not sad to see 'em gone."
He looked at me. "Do you understand what I mean?"

I told him I did, and for a moment we were quiet.

"I do wish Dorothy would've taken the boys like she'd said."

I thought about them following their father through the field to my house the night before, and I wondered if he'd made them stay behind because of me.

"No one knows how it started?" I asked.

Ezra shook his head. "I overheard one of the investigators say it was probably arson."

I felt my mouth fill with water and my stomach fold in on itself. My legs went weak, but I closed my eyes and the feeling passed.

"Arson?"

Ezra didn't speak.

"What do you think happened?" I asked. "Do you think someone—"

Ezra looked at me and I stopped.

His eyes were clear and sharp, and I was sure he could tell exactly what was going through my mind.

I kept quiet, and after a pause, Ezra turned back to the burned out trailer and said nothing.

42

When I got back to the house, I locked all the doors and windows and pulled the shades in every room. I didn't think this would keep her out, but it made me feel better. In time, once the pills kicked in, I knew she'd be gone completely, but until then I'd do whatever I could.

I sat in the corner on the floor where I had a clear view of the front door and squeezed the gun in my hand, clicking the safety off then on then off.

If Jessica came through, I'd be ready.

I knew she was out there. I could hear her footsteps on the porch, the boards moaning under her weight. Sometimes I'd see her shadow pass under the door and I'd hear her voice, whispering to herself, quiet, so I couldn't hear.

Other times she'd want me to hear. Then her voice would become loud and I'd hear every word.

She'd say the most horrible things.

. . .

The phone rang.

It was Liz.

She wouldn't let me explain.

"Just when I thought you were getting better, you go and pull something like this," she said. "Do you have any idea how much that window is going to cost?"

"Cost?"

I knew she was doing her best to keep her voice calm, but I also knew it was a struggle for her. I figured her mother was with her, listening.

"Yes, Dexter, *cost*," she said. "Money, that we don't have, and that my mother definitely doesn't have."

I didn't say anything.

"Why would you do something like this?"

My forehead itched, and I absently scratched at it with the barrel of my gun. When I realized what I was doing, I leaned forward and set the gun on the table.

"Are you still taking your meds? Were you ever taking them at all?"

"Yes," I said. "I'm taking them."

"I'm not sure I believe you."

"They take a while to kick in," I said. "You know that."

"They only take a few days. How long have you been taking them?"

I paused, then said, "Where were you yesterday? I waited for you at the docks."

"The search party? I decided not to go."

"I told your mother I'd meet you."

"You were down there?"

"Did she tell you?"

"Tell me what?"

"That I was waiting for you. Did she tell you I called or not?"

"I didn't see her yesterday. She didn't have a chance to tell me."

"So, she didn't tell you?"

Liz was quiet for a moment, then said, "Have you thought about talking to a doctor again? I don't think the pills are working anymore."

"I told you they take a while."

"But—"

"I just started them today," I said. "I was going to start them when I told you, but I couldn't make myself do it. I thought I could fight it."

"*Jesus*, Dexter."

We were both silent.

I heard a TV in the background; then Liz said, "Are you having the blackouts again?"

I told her I was, then paused. "I'm scared, Liz."

"You don't have any reason to be scared," she said. "You started the pills again, just give it some time."

I shook my head, didn't speak.

"I'll come over tonight and stay with you. We'll do it together and you'll be fine."

"No," I said. "Don't come over."

Liz ignored me.

"Once you feel better, we'll go to Archway and talk to Dr. Conner. Just to make sure things are back to the way they should be."

"I can't go back to Archway."

"Not to stay," she said. "Just to talk—"

"No."

She paused, then said, "We can talk when I get there. We don't have to make a decision now."

"I don't want you here," I said. "It's not safe."

"Not safe?"

For a moment I didn't say anything; then the tears came, snaking down my cheeks.

"Dexter?"

I couldn't speak.

"Dexter?" Liz's voice was soft, calming. "Did something happen?"

I looked up toward the front door. Jessica was standing outside. I could see her shadow moving behind the stained glass.

She was speaking to me in Clara's voice.

"Yes," I said. "Something's happened."

Liz waited for me to go on.

When I did, I told her everything.

43

"I called for you, Daddy."

I leaned over the table and pressed the metal tines of the fork into my forehead. The handle was slippery, and several drops of blood pooled on the table beneath me.

The pain was white and hot and beautiful, but the voice stayed.

"They're mean to me here. They hurt me."

I closed my eyes and pressed harder.

"Help me, Daddy, please."

"Stop it," I said. "Stop it. Stop."

It didn't stop. I pressed harder.

I felt blood cover my fingers, and pressed harder.

"Why won't you help?"

The fork slipped, and the metal tines tore through the skin, ripping away flesh, scraping against bone.

The pain was electric.

I jumped up, screaming, blood running in streams down my face, blinding me, filling my nose, my mouth.

The voice continued.

"Why, Daddy?"

I wiped the blood from my eyes, grabbed my gun from the table, and turned toward the door.

Jessica's shadow moved away.

The voice stopped.

· · ·

I leaned over the sink and pressed the dishtowel against my forehead. The pain split through my skull and radiated down my spine. I felt my legs waver. Darkness crept in from the sides of my vision, and I braced myself against the counter, waiting for it to pass.

When it did, I ran the water in the sink, soaked the towel, and tried again. The result was the same, but I forced myself to continue.

The fork had shredded my skin, and the blood wasn't slowing. The pain felt like ice drilling into my head.

I stood over the sink until the dishtowel soaked through red. I dropped it on the floor, then crossed into the hallway toward the bathroom.

I took the hand towel off the rack and ran it under the cold water. When I shut off the water, I looked at myself in the cracked mirror. I didn't recognize my reflection.

It wasn't the blood or the scabs or the way my skin hung loose and gray on my skull. It was my eyes. They weren't mine.

I made myself look away.

I held the towel against my head, and this time the pain wasn't as bad. I gave it a minute, then moved down the hall toward the living room. I set the gun on the coffee table and leaned back on the couch and tried to stop the roar in my head.

. . .

I heard the low rumble of tires on gravel and opened my eyes.

"Liz?"

I'd told her not to come, but I should've known she would anyway. I sat up and pulled the towel away from my forehead. The skin stuck and ripped in several places. Fresh blood started to flow, but nowhere near as much as before.

I pushed myself off the couch and crossed to the window. I pulled back the curtain and looked out.

Greg's cruiser sat at the end of the driveway.

She'd told him.

I waited for the panic to hit, but it never came. All I felt was a cold sense of relief. I even smiled.

Greg stayed in the cruiser for a while, talking on the radio, before opening the door and stepping out. When he did, he slid his hat on his head and stared up at the house.

I let the curtains close then stepped back from the glass. When I looked out again, Greg had moved away from the cruiser and started walking toward the break in the rows.

I watched him until he disappeared around the corner, then closed the curtains. As I did, I saw movement from the front of the porch. I pulled the curtains back again and saw Jessica crawling out from under the stairs. She stood and walked into the field.

I ran to the door, opened it, then stopped.

What was I going to do?

I stepped back inside and closed the door. The house was quiet and still. I took my gun from the coffee table and stood at the window, staring out at the break in the rows, waiting.

A few minutes later, Greg came out of the field. He had his hat off and was waving it in front of his face like a fan. When he got to the cruiser, he dropped the hat on the roof and opened the driver's side door and took out the radio and started taking. I couldn't hear what he was saying, but I had a pretty good idea.

Then I saw another car turn into the driveway. Liz. She parked behind the cruiser and got out. Greg hung up the radio and walked down to meet her. The conversation looked heated. I decided it might be better to go out and try to calm things down. All of this was my fault, and I figured I should face up, come clean in person.

I stepped back from the window just as Jessica came out of the corn, her black dress torn and caked with mud.

She crossed the yard toward Greg and Liz, moving fast.

I didn't want to see, but I couldn't turn away. I knew I had to do something to warn them, so I slammed my hand against the glass and shouted.

Greg and Liz both looked up at the window and for a second, just before Jessica got to them, our eyes met.

I let the curtain drop and backed away until I hit the wall, then slid to the ground, my knees pressing into my chest.

I listened for screaming, but all I could hear was an explosion of noise. Nothing was coming through, and I felt tears slide down my face. I stayed on the ground staring at the front door, waiting for her to come up the steps.

It didn't take long.

Her shadow passed behind the stained glass. I raised the gun.

"Go away," I said, but it came out as a whisper.

I saw the doorknob turn and rattle. Locked.

I pushed myself to my feet and aimed at the shadow through the glass. "Go away." Louder this time.

For a moment there was nothing; then something heavy struck the door. I jumped.

"Go away!" I was screaming.

She struck the door again, and I saw the wood frame splinter.

I squeezed the gun and fired. Again and again.

When I stopped, the glass in the door had broken away. I could see daylight through the holes.

In the distance, I heard Liz screaming.

I crossed the room and opened the door. When I saw the blood I stepped back. Greg was lying on the porch, a thick red stain spreading under him. His mouth opened and closed, but there was no sound. His eyes were empty.

Jessica stood over him.

"You did it," she said. "Finally."

I shook my head.

Liz was running up the driveway. Jessica turned toward her, then back to me and said, "Just one more."

I slammed the door and backed down the hallway to the bathroom. I went in, turned on the fluorescent light, and sat on the floor beside the toilet, staring at the gun.

I could hear Liz in the house, running toward the kitchen. I could hear her pick up the phone and tell someone that Greg had been shot. That I'd shot him.

I looked up at the bathroom door and thought of Liz on the other side. I didn't know if there were any bullets left or not, but I only needed one.

Maybe I'd get lucky.

I got up, bracing myself against the sink.

The mirror was empty.

I stood for a minute, until I felt balanced, then put the barrel of the pistol under my chin and pulled the trigger.

44

The sky slides above me in a scream of blue and white and yellow. I close my eyes and let it pass. The voices come to me, again and again. And then they are gone, and all I hear is the slow tumble of the river.

I'm on my back, drifting with the current.

When I open my eyes, I'm staring into the sun.

Someone leans over me, shines a light, and whispers something I can't hear.

Then they are gone and I'm alone.

Floating in the haze.

. . .

"Mr. McCray? Can you hear me?"

The voice is deep and it pulls at me. I want to answer, but the river moves too fast.

"Do you know where you are?"

I try to speak, but the pain vibrates through the center of my head and fills everything. Still, I force my legs to move under me, and when my feet touch the ground I stand.

The river is gone.

I'm in my field, waist deep in the corn. The sun rests low on the horizon, and above me the sky weeps a depthless red.

In the distance, I hear cheering.

There is no wind, but the corn bends and moves around me as if alive. I turn and look for a space between the rows, but there is no path, nowhere to go, just a sea of unending green.

The cheering grows louder, and I hear something else underneath, grinding and sharp, like metal ripping in a hollow room.

I scan the horizon and at first there is nothing. Then something moves in the corn, slow at first, but gaining speed, splitting the rows, coming toward me.

I turn and run, but the corn bends, thick and strong, holding me in place.

"Dexter?"

Liz's voice.

I try to call out, but the corn moves in and I can't breathe.

The grinding noise grows louder, and the air turns thick and hot and carries the poison-sweet smell of burning oil.

Black smoke covers me and I don't turn around.

I know what's coming.

And it has teeth.

45

I had a dream someone was in the house...

I open my eyes. The room is bright.

Liz is sitting in a red plastic chair at the foot of the bed. She has a book on her lap, and when she looks up and sees me, she smiles.

Her eyes are red and swollen.

I try to speak, but my mouth won't open.

Liz closes her book and comes to the side of the bed. She leans close and takes my hand. "Hi, Dexter," she says.

I try to say something, anything, but she shakes her head and says, "Don't talk, OK?"

She stares at me for a moment longer, then slides her hand away from mine. "I'll find the doctor."

She turns toward the door, and I try to call for her. What comes out sounds thin and weak.

Liz turns and touches her fingers to her lips and begins to cry.

. . .

The doctor tells me I got lucky.

He says the bullet passed through the soft spot under

my chin and came out my left eye socket along with most of my left eye. On the way, it tore away part of my tongue and jawbone and shredded my sinus.

He tells me that if the bullet had entered my skull, it wouldn't have had the velocity to pass through the bone and would've wound up spinning inside my head like a marble in a bowl.

"People live through things like that all the time," he says. "More often than not, in a vegetative state." He pauses, and then adds, "A .22 is a very dangerous gun, in that regard."

I try to speak, forgetting the wires in my jaw.

The doctor hands me a notepad and a pencil.

I use it to ask about Greg.

He tells me it was touch and go for a while, but the surgery went well and Greg will be fine in a few weeks.

He says I fired eight shots but only hit Greg with two. The first in the bicep, not too serious. The second in the chest, very serious. The second bullet clipped a section of his heart before embedding itself in his lung and collapsing it.

"If it hadn't been for your wife thinking fast and calling for help, he certainly would've died." The doctor smiles. "Both of you, more than likely."

Liz is a hero.

She's been by my side the entire time. At first, all she did was cry, but now she's better.

Most of the time, I sit in bed and scribble questions on the notepad, asking about Greg, how he's doing. She keeps me updated.

I tried to explain things to her one time, but she held up a hand and wouldn't look at my notes.

"He knows," she said. "And he understands."

I asked her if she felt the same way, but she didn't answer, just looked toward the window and the bright day passing outside.

Silent.

It's nice when she's around.

· · ·

No one came to question me about Jessica. When I asked Liz, she told me not to bring it up.

I did anyway.

Finally, she told me that after the news came out, Megan from the café stepped forward and admitted to being out in the grove with Jessica and her boyfriend. She said they'd all taken some pills they'd found in her mother's cabinet, and that Jessica had just collapsed and stopped breathing.

"They panicked," Liz said. "Panicked and ran."

She looked away and was silent. I knew what she was thinking. I was thinking it, too.

When Liz spoke again, she said, "Jessica had some kind of heart condition. No one knew about it, and it didn't mix with the medicine. That was all."

I had more questions, but Liz stopped me.

"We can't talk about this," she said. "Not yet."

I asked her when.

"Soon."

We were both quiet for a while. Then I asked about the fire at the Tollivers' trailer.

Liz looked confused, and I wrote the story out for her, handing her page after page.

"I don't know anything about this," she said. "But I'll ask if you'd like."

I told her I would.

• • •

There are no mirrors in my room. The nurses say I can't see anything but bandages anyway, but if I really want to know, I looked just like Claude Raines in the old *Invisible Man* movie.

I tell them I've never seen it.

Earlier, the doctor came by to tell me I'm being transferred to Archway in a couple days, as soon as the bandages are off. I didn't take the news very well, but he assured me there would be no shock treatments.

"They stopped doing those years ago," he said. "These days, it's just medication and therapy and rest."

That sounded fine.

• • •

Liz talked to one of the deputies in Greg's office and they told her they'd arrested Ezra Hays for the fire that killed Frank and Dorothy Tolliver and their two boys.

"He just walked in and confessed," she said. "Hard to believe a nice man like Ezra would do something like that."

She was right. It was hard to believe.

I took out the notepad and asked her if the deputy was sure no one else started the fire.

She said he was positive.

I wrote that Ezra could be lying.

"Why would he lie about this?" She shook her head. "No, he's telling the truth. Apparently he was so upset because the wife and the kids were home that he decided to come forward."

I nodded and wrote that they were supposed to be out of town.

"How do you know that?"

I told her about my conversation with Ezra.

"Did he tell you they were stealing from him?"

I nodded.

"Did he tell you Frank Tolliver beat him up and threatened to kill him after Ezra confronted him?"

I shook my head. If that was true, Ezra's pride wouldn't have allowed him to admit that to anyone. Old or not, the man was once a war hero.

"Ezra's in his eighties. I don't blame him a bit for going after that man. Most people feel the same way. Frank Tolliver made a lot of enemies." Liz turned toward the window and shook her head. "It's too bad, though. Everyone is just devastated over those kids, especially Ezra."

I looked down.

"There's even been talk about bringing in a lawyer from Chicago who thinks he can get him out of the whole thing."

I asked her again if they were sure it was him.

Liz stared at me for a while, then said, "Do you think you started that fire?"

I closed the notebook, didn't answer.

"Dexter." She leaned close. "You didn't kill Frank Tolliver. Do you understand?"

I thought about it, nodded, then looked away.

. . .

The doctor is taking the bandages off this afternoon, and I've been warned about how it'll look.

"It might be a shock," he said. "So be prepared."

I'm not scared. If anything, I'm excited. I don't think I'll like what I see, but I'm not going to be shocked, either.

When we were kids, Greg's father had a series of books on World War I, and inside were all kinds of pictures of injured soldiers. Greg and I would sit on the floor and go over the photos, looking for the most gruesome ones.

Many of the soldiers were missing noses and eyes and jaws. Some had their lips melted away by mustard gas or entire sections of their faces blown off after being shot while peeking out of trenches.

I figure I'll look something like that.

If Greg still has those books, maybe I'll ask him to bring them by sometime so we can compare.

Maybe not.

I'd like to talk to Greg before they move me, but I doubt I'll get the chance. Hopefully he'll come see me at Archway so I can tell him I'm sorry.

Liz says he understands, but I need to be sure.

He's always been like family to me, almost as much as Liz or Clara, and that's something you keep close for as long as you can.

• • •

Liz won't talk to me about our future together, and I'm not going to push her. I don't feel a big need to know what's going to happen. I suppose a part of me already knows, and that's fine.

We had a lot of good years together, more than most marriages, and I hate to see them end, but the truth is they ended a while ago, when Clara died.

It just took us some time to notice.

Still, for a while things were good, and I can walk away knowing that no matter what else happened, and no matter what other people thought, we were happy.

All three of us.

And when you have that, no matter how long it lasts, you've been blessed.

• • •

I won't look in a mirror. I've had enough of them.

The nurse tried to hold one up for me when the doctor took the bandages off, but I looked away.

"It's OK," the doctor said, touching the nurse's arm. "There's no rush."

It didn't matter. I didn't need a mirror. All I had to do was look at Liz's face.

She didn't even have to say a word.

• • •

The van arrives to take me to Archway, and I change into a set of clothes Liz brought from home.

I can't take anything else except what I'm wearing, and when I get there, they'll take those things, too.

I don't mind losing my clothes, but I don't want them to take Clara's bracelet. Liz said she'd hold onto it for me, but I'm going to keep it for as long as I can.

I want it close.

Liz wheels me out to the parking lot then leans over and kisses my cheek. She tells me she'll be up in a couple days, once I get settled.

She doesn't cry, and I don't blame her. I can only imagine what people are saying about me in town, what she has had to go through.

I'm helped into the van, and when we pull away I don't look back. Once we are on the highway and out of town, I lean my head against the window and stare out at the blur of trees passing along the road.

Eventually, the trees fall away to fields and hills and the occasional empty house.

All of it passes.

I watch the scenery for a while. Then my vision shifts and I see myself reflected in the glass, my face as thin as a daytime moon. It makes me smile, and I can't look away.

It's like seeing a ghost.

about the author

John Rector is a prize-winning short story writer and the author of the novel *The Cold Kiss*, optioned for a feature film now in development. He lives in Omaha, Nebraska.

acknowledgments

This book would not exist if it wasn't for the support of three people: My wife, Amy, who believed from day one and has never stopped; my friend, Sean Doolittle, who graciously answered every writing and publishing question I could throw at him; and my agent, Allan Guthrie, who took a chance on me and this book and who has worked tirelessly ever since. I'd also like to thank my early readers: Eric Stark, Stephen Sommerville, Vincent Van Allen, Edmund R. Schubert, and Sunil Sadanand for their time and their input. And finally, I'd like to thank Terry Goodman and everyone at Amazon Publishing for breathing new life into this dark little tale.